FAKE

TAKE FOUNTAIN

A NOVEL

ADAM NOVAK

ENTER THE WORLD OF TAKE FOUNTAIN...
ALL YOU HAVE TO LOSE ARE YOUR ILLUSIONS

A GENUINE RARE BIRD BOOK
LOS ANGELES, CALIF.

This is a Genuine Rare Bird Book

A Rare Bird Book | Rare Bird Books
453 South Spring Street, Suite 531
Los Angeles, CA 90013
rarebirdbooks.com

FIRST HARDCOVER EDITION

Set in Goudy Old Style
Printed in the United States

10 9 8 7 6 5 4 3 2 1

Publisher's Cataloging-in-Publication data

Novak, Adam.
Take fountain : a novel / by Adam Novak.
p. cm.
ISBN 9781940207759

1. Podcasts—Fiction. 2. Cold cases (Criminal investigation)—Fiction. 3. Murder—Investigation—Fiction. 4. Motion picture industry—California—Los Angeles. 5. Hollywood (Los Angeles, Calif.)—Fiction. 6. Suspense—Fiction. I. Title.

PS3614.O9253 T35 2015

813.6—dc23

A laptop computer is reported stolen from the Santa Clarita Police Department evidence room.

In Los Angeles, Rare Bird Books receives an e-mail containing a folder titled *Take Fountain* with a disturbing interview between screenwriter Dollars Muttlan and Omniscience script guru Larry Mersault.

The transcript of that interview is approved for publication by the Santa Clarita Chief of Police.

About Larry Mersault

b. November 21, 1968 – d. March 15, 2013

As a film student at USC, Larry Mersault played a ruthless drug dealer in John Singleton's senior thesis video of *Boyz N The Hood*, which prepared him for the motion picture industry.

His 2008 novel, *Schadenfreude*, was called "a gripping thriller" by *Midwest Book Review*.

Head of the story department at powerhouse talent agency Omniscience for two decades, Mersault was named by *Smash Cut* magazine as one of the "Top 100 People You Need to Know" in Hollywood.

About Dollars Muttlan

Dollars Muttlan wrote the major motion picture *Warlords of Arkadia*, released in 2003 by Paramount Pictures.

In 2009, he wrote, starred, produced, and directed the award-winning independent film *The Last Wedding*, which premiered on Time Warner Cable VOD.

An adjunct professor of screenwriting at College of the Canyons, his current whereabouts remain unknown.

[recording begins]

Dollars: Is this thing on?

Mersault: It's your show, Dollars.

Dollars: Tell us the best advice you ever got.

Mersault: First of all, thank you for inviting me to speak to your online screenwriting class and thanks to all of you out there for listening. Twenty years ago, I met Paul Newman in Connecticut at Uncle Ray's house for Thanksgiving. There was a pool table in the basement and I was shooting nine ball by myself waiting for the turkey when Uncle Ray's best friend Paul Newman came down the stairs with a beer and chalked up a cue stick. I asked Newman if he wanted to break. He nodded, and took a gulp straight from the can. Newman broke, and then the two ball, the eight ball, and the five ball fell in. The movie star had no idea I played pool every night in LA at a dive bar against a one-armed Vietnam vet called the Vulture who would let you beat him for a Michelob then place a crumpled twenty-dollar bill in the side pocket and hustle you for all your money. Newman chugged his Budweiser and missed his shot. I sank the one ball and the three ball and he asked me what I did for a living and I told him I was in the movie business and he said, "Tough racket." I said I read scripts for Omniscience and he said, "I used to be represented by them, now I'm with Ovitz." I knocked in the four ball and the six ball and he asked me if I wanted to know the key to the movie business and I said, "Absolutely." I banked in the seven ball and he said, "Longevity," and I thought to myself, *That's it? That's your nugget?* I drilled the nine ball in the corner and said, "I just beat Fast Eddie Felson," and Newman said, "Rack 'em," and I never won another game until it was time to eat the bird.

Dollars: Longevity? Interesting nugget.

Mersault: Newman was right. I'm living proof.

Dollars: How did you get named by *Smash Cut* magazine as one of the "Top 100 People You Need to Know" in Hollywood?

Mersault: To get on that list you have to give a speech in front of three hundred aspiring writers at a *Smash Cut* screenwriting convention.

Dollars: Elaborate, please.

Mersault: The publisher needed a keynote speaker at the magazine's pitchfest event where industry people agreed to hear five-minute pitches from desperados around the world. Some ridiculously famous screenwriter had bailed on *Smash Cut* and the publisher asked me if I would step in at the last minute and do a Q&A about the state of the union of the industry. When I got to the Roosevelt Hotel, the air conditioning was on the fritz, and everyone walking around the lobby looked violently happy. I was the only one wearing a suit and tie. I entered the Lincoln Ballroom and saw three hundred people sitting in rows listening to director Eben Gillespie showing clips of his Sylvester Stallone movie *Officer Down* and discussing his creative process at the convention. Somebody told me I was next and when I bounded up to the stage I was met with total silence. I began by telling the room I'd had some trepidation coming as a script reader to speak to a room full of writers about the business. I said it must have felt the same way when a Christian first stepped into the Coliseum. No one laughed. I sensed their hostility and told them, "Wow, I didn't realize the hotel bathrobes came with hoods." A few chuckles. Then I lit into them like a fiery Baptist preacher and told them blaming the script reader for their failure was not acceptable. I had agreed to speak at this convention for one reason and one reason only: I wanted every one of them to win. How many scripts have they written? Did they think this business was easy? What did they think buyers were looking for in a screenplay? I told them I was there to answer their questions until they had none, and then I would get off the stage. I told them a little bit about myself, but for the most part everyone there was handed a microphone and each asked me a question which I did my very best to answer, and if I didn't have an answer, if I didn't know where somebody could find international distribution for their paraplegic zombie film, I said, "I have no fucking idea." I answered their questions for two hours straight. When I left the stage they were still applauding. In the parking lot of the Roosevelt Hotel, a woman thrust her thick screenplay into my chest and said, "Please,

please help me. I'm the next Vietnamese Billy Bob Thornton. Will you read my script?" The publisher was so impressed with my talk she declared I was one of the "Top 100 People You Need To Know" in the movie business.

Dollars: In the *Smash Cut* article, it says one of the highlights of your career was Woody Allen thanking you for finding him a script?

Mersault: Omniscience signed Woody Allen and the first thing he said to his new agent was, "Is my old agent still there?" A legend at age ninety-two, Methuselah Gwartz went to work every day in his office on the first floor. Whenever I saw an ambulance in front of the Omniscience building my immediate reaction was always, "Gwartz!" Anyway, Woody Allen wanted to do a movie where he would only act, preferably a comedy, for a payday. Woody turned down some suggestions, expressed interest in starring in a Dreamworks movie but that picture was in development and wasn't anywhere near production, so his agent asked me if I had any great scripts on the shelf. I suggested a dark comedy I'd read years ago called *Rest in Pieces* that Polygram Pictures had developed for Julien

Temple to direct after he did *Earth Girls Are Easy*. Nicolas Cage was attached at one point to play a butcher who chopped up his cheating wife and buried her pieces in Mexico. Unfortunately for Cage, his wife's severed hand is discovered by an old, blind Mexican woman who trips over the hand and miraculously regains her sight when she stands up. Convinced the appendage is the hand of the Virgin Mary, she takes the hand, middle finger still extended at her killer, back to her village where a shrine is built and quickly thereafter more miracles start to occur in the village: the sick are healed, the illiterate can read, acne goes away, and word of mouth spreads, creating a tourist frenzy. The local priest, enduring a crisis of faith (while enjoying a torrid affair with the town's stunning prostitute), starts to believe again in the existence of God when the butcher returns to the Mexican village to steal the severed hand since it is the only evidence linking him to the heinous crime. Shenanigans ensue. The priest was going to be played by Raul Julia, but he died of a stroke and the movie never got made. I gave the script of *Rest in Pieces* to our director client Alfonso Arau, who made *Like Water for Chocolate*, because his agent asked me to find Alfonso a contained comedy that could be shot in Mexico for two million dollars. I got a phone call from Alfonso saying, "Thank you for the script. It is no longer with Polygram Pictures. I am now in preproduction." Alfonso Arau then received a phone call from Woody Allen's agent suggesting Woody wanted to play the butcher. Alfonso's blasphemous no-budget movie became this hulk of an independent Woody Allen comedy financed through sold-out foreign presales around the world with the US distribution rights available for auction when the picture was completed. Woody was set to play the butcher for three weeks and casting began for the other roles. Everybody's first choice, Andy Garcia, passed. The producers settled on David Schwimmer to play the Catholic priest even though he was from TV and happened to be of the Jewish persuasion. Alfonso convinced the stunning Bond Girl from *The World Is Not Enough*, Maria Grazia Cucinotta, to play the lovely prostitute and Cheech Marin agreed to play the Mayor. When the start date was announced, Woody Allen and his wife, Soon-Yi, came to Brentwood for a party in his honor, which I was invited to attend. This was truly an A-list party, Barbara Streisand and James Brolin canoodling on an outdoor couch, and a long line of stars and agents waiting to congratulate Woody Allen on his upcoming movie. My date and I were about to get in line when my classmate from film school, John Singleton, tapped me on the shoulder and asked, "Larry, what are you doing here?" We bumped fists and I asked him, "What are you doing here?" Our dates looked at each other with seething hatred. We laughed and then Woody Allen's agent pulled me away from Singleton and his date, saying loud enough for John to hear: "Larry, this way, Woody wants to meet you." So the agent brought us to the very front of this long receiving line to meet Woody Allen and Soon-Yi. The agent told Woody I was the one who found the screenplay and Woody reacted like he'd been shot, touching his chest while shaking my hand, telling his wife, "Soon-Yi, this is the guy, thank you, that was the most subversive script anyone's ever sent me."

Dollars: Your date wanted to jump in the bushes with you. John Singleton probably wanted to kill you. How come I never heard of this movie?

Mersault: Eight people saw it and they were divided. Alfonso hired the Oscar-winning cinematographer Vittorio Storaro to shoot the picture. It was a tight shooting schedule and since most of the budget went to Woody Allen's fee there wasn't much money left to put on the screen. Cheech described the movie as "The best ingredients in the world mixed in a cup of vomit." Some of the romantic moonlight compositions between Schwimmer, the priest, and Cucinotta, the prostitute, were so beautiful they looked like Rembrandt paintings. Some shots were out of focus. The sets looked cheap. Schwimmer was miscast. The only actor who really shined in this terrible movie, the one hilarious performance, was Woody Allen. The financier sold *Rest in Pieces* to Cinemax, where it premiered into oblivion.

Dollars: If you were stranded on a desert island with a volleyball named Wilson and one script to read, what would it be?

Mersault: *True Romance.* I remember when I first read it, how my hair felt about it, and to this day, I can pick up Quentin Tarantino's script, revisit any part, and it still holds up magnificently. Even the title page was different, it said: "When you're tired of relationships, try a romance." Omniscience signed Quentin before anybody knew who he was, so I got to read all of his screenplays, and this was before *Reservoir Dogs* had even come out yet. At the time, my father, Richard Mersault, was in business with Walter Yetnikoff, the legendary head of CBS Records who had signed Springsteen and Michael Jackson, and Yetnikoff and Dad were starting a movie company together. The music mogul had just left CBS Records and couldn't work in the record business for two years because of a noncompete clause in his contract. Dad and Yetnikoff came to Los Angeles with a P&A fund to pitch companies that needed money to pay for prints and advertising in order to theatrically distribute their movies, and one of the companies that had a slate of finished movies but no money to release them was a company called Live Entertainment. Dad and I went to Morton's on a Monday night with an executive at Live who invited a movie star to join us: Emilio Estevez. While Dad and the executive from Live were talking shop, I was sitting next to Otto from *Repo Man*, telling him how my mom went to UCLA film school and her professor was Peter McCarthy, who produced *Repo Man*. I told Emilio I was a story analyst at Omniscience and we talked about this script I had just read called *Freejack* (Emilio would star in the picture years later for Morgan Creek). By the end of the meal, Dad and the Live executive agreed to set a screening at the Carolco building on Sunset so they could consider their slate of movies for the P&A fund. Outside Morton's, Emilio asked me what was the best script I'd ever read and I said *True Romance*. Emilio suggested Omniscience messenger the script to him in Malibu but he told me under no circumstances was I to put his name on the envelope. He suggested I use the name Gordon Bombay which I realized later was the name of his character from Disney's *Mighty Ducks* franchise. A week later I got a call from Emilio who said he loved Quentin's script but he had this hockey movie in the can for a family audience and couldn't see himself doing *True Romance*. At the Carolco screening room, Dad and Yetnikoff and I watched an entire weekend of bad movies that Live had financed: *A Gnome Named Gnorm*, starring Anthony Michael Hall, about a cop who's partnered with a troll; *Iron Eagle III*, with Louis Gossett, Jr.–pretty much unwatchable; *The Dark Wind*, directed by acclaimed documentarian Errol Morris–I think Yetnikoff took a power nap halfway through that one; *Light Sleeper*, a new film directed by *Taxi Driver* writer Paul Schrader, starring Willem Dafoe, about an insomniac NYC drug dealer–better than the other movies but had no audience. I waved my finger in the air, mimicking Dad and Yetnikoff, who had made the gesture to the projectionist all weekend, and the last film of the Live slate flickered on the screen: *Reservoir Dogs*. When the movie was over, Yetnikoff and Dad were so excited they went back to the executive at Live and declared they were not interested in *A Gnome Named Gnorm* or *Iron Eagle III*, they wanted to put up the P&A to support a theatrical release for *Reservoir Dogs*. The executive turned them down, saying they couldn't cherry-pick Quentin's movie, which was about to premiere at the nineteen ninety-two Sundance Film Festival. They would have to take all of the Live movies. Everybody knows Miramax picked up *Reservoir Dogs* for distribution, but what nobody knows is Dad and Yetnikoff had a meeting with Harvey and Bob Weinstein and in that meeting Harvey told Yetnikoff he thought the world of him and suggested a "Walter Yetnikoff Presents" credit at the front of the film and a producer credit for my father. Live objected to this suggestion. Dad and Yetnikoff went to Sundance thinking they were going to be credited with championing the festival's great discovery, only to be told at the *Reservoir Dogs* Sundance party it wasn't going to happen. Paul Schrader was at that party discussing *Light Sleeper* with my Dad when Roger Avary came up to them and said he was best friends with Quentin Tarantino and that Quentin was too shy to ask his idol, Paul Schrader, what he thought of *Reservoir Dogs*, so he put Roger up to the task. Schrader told Roger Avary two things: one, "Tell Quentin he liked the film very much"; two, "When Quentin is back in LA he should pick up the phone and call Larry Mersault at Omniscience." Roger Avary, who later shared the best screenplay Oscar for *Pulp Fiction* with his best friend, reported what Paul Schrader said and a week later Quentin Tarantino called me at my office and we had a fantastic half-hour phone call about our mutual love for the nineteen seventy-nine horror film *Phantasm*.

CRIME WAVE SURFERS
Screenplay by Rand Quevera

COMMENTS: Shocking pulp fiction presented in a masterful, innovative screenplay that defies convention and offers up gallows humor with blood-soaked violence. Sort of like a trilogy of short stories, this is actually one narrative with overlapping characters. Young fella RENO figures in all of them. One story has Reno going out with crime boss wife HAYLEY when she accidentally overdoses on heroin. Reno and his smack dealer have to inject her heart with adrenaline–if she dies, Reno dies. She makes it. Another story has a prizefighter named SHARIF on the run from the crime boss. Sharif has to risk his life to retrieve a family heirloom from his apartment. Instead, he murders Reno, who's been sent to kill him. Third story has Reno and his buddy GOMEZ shooting a guy's brains out in their car. And then racing against the clock to clean the blood and bone and dispose of the body. These three tales are bookended by a pair of armed robbers named CHRISTMAS and PUDDY TAT, who hold up a Denny's and meet Reno and Gomez in a Mexican standoff that ends the script on a hugely satisfying note. By mixing up the narrative, Reno can get killed in the middle—and still walk out alive at the end of the standoff. Script's strength lies in its conversational, hilarious dialogue, and memorable cast of cool characters. In part to its unusual structure, narrative is consistently entertaining, whether it's Hayley and Reno having a get-to-know-each-other dinner or the intense scenes of violence that seem to follow the characters like their shadows. The intensity of this crime drama is definitely not for the faint of heart (i.e. there's a rape sequence in a pawn shop that's so brutal and excessive it makes the Ned Beatty scene from DELIVERANCE look like ALADDIN). The excesses may be shocking, but the characters and dialogue and script's fiendishly funny sense of humor should override our instinct to look away. Casting for this dark material looks enticing, with many memorable roles here for our clients.

Dollars: Other than Quentin Tarantino, whose scripts did you worship?

Mersault: Charlie Kaufman. Just like there was Quentin, and then there was everybody else, there was *Being John Malkovich*—and there was everything else. I was in a staff meeting when the agent who covered Columbia Pictures told the room that Charlie Kaufman was late in delivering his assignment adapting Susan Orlean's book *The Orchid Thief* for Jonathan Demme. Then I heard Columbia was not happy that he had written himself into the story, credited half the script to Donald Kaufman, who didn't exist, and made it about a fat, balding screenwriter named Charlie Kaufman who becomes obsessed with Susan Orlean and finds out she's having a drug-fueled affair with the orchid thief of the book's title.

Dollars: Charlie Kaufman received an Academy Award for *Eternal Sunshine of the Spotless Mind.* Why do you think that won the Oscar for best screenplay and not *Malkovich* or *Adaptation*?

Mersault: Because it had a third act. I was the one who brought that script into the agency. I woke up one morning at the Santa Monica apartment of my girlfriend (who I went to the Oscars with that year) and in the kitchen there was this guy drinking fresh coffee at the breakfast table. Obviously he'd spent the night with my girlfriend's roommate, because, like me, he was in his boxer shorts and T-shirt and we both had these smiles laid on our faces. I poured a mug of moe and introduced myself. He asked me if last night was a hole in one. I smiled, then he asked me what I did for a living. I told him, and he smiled. I asked him what he did to make rent and he said he had just been promoted to head of the story department at a rival agency called Ragnarök. We kept having morning coffee together in this Santa Monica apartment until he broke up with the roommate, but we became best friends who spoke every day and I watched him leave Ragnarök and become a producer which is what he really wanted to be doing all along. Before he left, my friend invited me to Ragnarök's five-year anniversary party at some club on Robertson Boulevard in West Hollywood. John Singleton came up to me that night and said, "What the fuck are you doing here?" Anyway, it was my Ragnarök counterpart who gave me a copy of *Eternal Sunshine of the Spotless Mind.*

Dollars: You went to the Academy Awards?

Mersault: That year the Oscars were held in the Shrine Auditorium near USC where I had my graduation ceremony and afterward all the graduates received a movie poster with a yellow brick road designed like a ribbon of seventy millimeter film honoring the USC School of Cinema-Television class of nineteen ninety. When you have to go to the bathroom at the Oscars there's a seat-filler dressed like a guest who takes your place, so when the show resumes there's never an empty seat. There was a commercial break after the in memoriam clips and I was standing at the urinal facing a framed movie poster of a yellow brick road in the shape of a seventy millimeter filmstrip honoring the USC School of Cinema-Television class of nineteen ninety and in that moment I realized where I was, how I got there, and felt very fortunate.

Dollars: I went to the Razzies for *Warlords of Arkadia* to pick up my Golden Raspberry award for worst screenplay. I had just broken up with my girlfriend and she was really pissed off. When I got the call that I had won, I was told if I wanted the trophy I had to attend the ceremony and give a thank you speech. I had this friend of a friend who was a model, an absolute ten, abused as a child, used to men buying her gifts. I remember trying to date her when she asked me to buy her a dog for like five hundred bucks, and in that moment I realized I could not afford this high-maintenance chick so I said let's just be friends. I invited her to accompany me to the Razzies and she looked smoking hot and we were just friends having a great time at this absurd event where I'm about to make a speech when my furious ex-girlfriend stormed over to us and screamed, "I knew you'd be here," causing this unbelievable scene and security escorted her out of the building while she gave us the finger with both hands. My foxy friend looked at me and said, "That was interesting." I accepted my Razzie award, posed for some pictures with Sandra Bullock, and as we were leaving I turned to the model and asked her if she wanted me to take her home and she looked at me and said, "Let's go to your place and fuck."

Mersault: And I thought I was blessed.

Dollars: I'd like to open up the class to questions. Text your question to thirty-three, seventy-seven, eighty-eight with hashtag Dollars and we'll put them on screen.

YOU PASSED ON MY SCRIPT
I'M GONNA KILL MYSELF

Mersault: Write another one.

[21]

HOW DO YOU KNOW WHEN YOU'VE GOT A GREAT SCRIPT?

Mersault: A good rule of thumb when something blows your mind: You read the script again and you still love it.

WHAT'S THE BEST WAY TO GET INTO HOLLYWOOD?

Mersault: Johnny Carson asked Bette Davis what was the best way for an aspiring actress to get into Hollywood and her advice was "Take Fountain."

Dollars: You said your Mom went to UCLA film school. Is that who we blame for getting you into this godforsaken business?

Mersault: My mother, Zenobia, was a child movie star growing up in Sweden. Her father, Soren, was a director who was supposed to go to Hollywood with Greta Garbo, but tragically Soren was killed on the set of his movie when a truck loaded with dynamite lost control and blew up. In nineteen eighty, Mom sent my brother Carlson and I to summer camp in New Hampshire so she could make movies at UCLA film school. Her sixteen millimeter short won best film and the winner got a job as a production assistant on a Brian De Palma movie called *Blow Out*. Mom invited us to visit her on set and we met John Travolta and the cinematographer Vilmos Zsigmond and producer Fred Caruso. It was the last year of the Carter presidency and Dad was working in the White House, so Mom left the shoot in Philadelphia to attend a state dinner and there was a receiving line where guests were announced before they met the President and first lady and my parents were talking to President Carter when John Travolta appeared in line and said, "Zenobia, what in the world are you doing here?" and the lowly production assistant said, "Hello John, may I introduce you to the First Lady and the President of the United States?" When *Blow Out* resumed shooting, Mom got dirty looks from the other production assistants who'd heard about the Travolta incident at the White

House and one of them welcomed my mom back with, “Hello Zenobia, slumming it are we?” After the movie wrapped, Mom joined the “Women in Film” organization, subscribed to *Variety* and *The Hollywood Reporter*, and took me to a screenwriting lecture at the Kennedy Center where I was the only boy in an auditorium full of women listening to Diane Thomas, who wrote *Romancing the Stone*. I read William Goldman’s *Adventures in the Screen Trade* and no longer wanted to go to Yale Law School like my father. I wanted to be a screenwriter.

Dollars: Wasn’t Diane Thomas the waitress at Gladstone’s who told Michael Douglas she had written a script and gave him *Romancing the Stone* from the trunk of her Toyota?

Mersault: The same Diane Thomas who was killed in a car crash in the brand new Porsche that Michael Douglas bought for her after the success of *Romancing the Stone*.

Dollars: The movie gods can be cruel. How old were you?

Mersault: Sixteen. After hearing Diane Thomas speak, Mom and I went to the Aspen Playwrights

Conference for a screenwriting seminar taught by Tracy Keenan Wynn, who wrote *The Longest Yard,* and Lorenzo Semple Jr., who wrote *The Parallax View.* Mom and I had an agreement we wouldn't tell anyone we were related. We arrived separately and sat away from each other in class. We learned how to write scenes and analyze movies and complete a short screenplay by the end of the summer. Everyone had to read their scenes out loud and because I loved slasher movies like *Halloween* my scripts always had somebody getting stabbed or disemboweled. When Mom finished reading her scene out loud to the class, I blew our cover and said, "That was awesome, Mom." This construction worker taking the class told her, "Larry's going to be a terrific screenwriter one day," and she said, "That, or a great butcher."

Dollars: Yale Law, UCLA film school, your DNA sounds amazing. Tell us about your very first screenplay.

Mersault: I noticed this *Variety* article about a project called *Handcarved Coffins* that Oscar-winner Michael Cimino was going to direct based on a nonfiction novella by Truman Capote. The project was languishing in development hell because Cimino had directed an expensive dud called *Heaven's Gate* that wiped out its studio, United Artists. *Variety* described *Handcarved Coffins* as a series of murders in a small town where before each victim dies they receive a miniature handcarved coffin with a picture of them inside. It was the most diabolical story I'd ever heard, better than any *Friday the 13th* movie, so at the age of seventeen I decided my first script would be an unauthorized adaptation of one of Hollywood's best unproduced projects and I would be the one who would finally get *Handcarved Coffins* made. My slasher version was probably unreadable, and the project remains unproduced. I started thinking about film schools and the only university that offered an undergraduate screenwriting degree was USC.

Dollars: When I applied to film school and got rejected, it was like–you didn't know anybody, you didn't get in.

Mersault: There were over a thousand applicants for twenty-six spots in USC's Filmic Writing Program. When I was applying, my Dad remembered his best friend from the Marine

Corps worked at USC, a guy named Bob Tanner, so Dad called him and Tanner arranged a tour of the film school for us. They hadn't spoken since Dad saved Bob's life at a steakhouse in Oceanside after Bob started choking and Dad reached down his throat to pull out the piece of meat. When Dad called about his son applying to USC, not only was Tanner the head of fundraising for the university, he was the guy who took George Lucas to a Trojan football game and at halftime convinced the creator of *Star Wars* to write a check for five million bucks and put his name on the film school.

Dollars: There's lucky, I suppose, and then, well, there's you.

Mersault: Absolutely. I've been blessed to have learned from some amazing screenwriters. My professors at USC were legends: Syd Field, blacklisted writer/director Abraham Polonsky (*Body and Soul*), and Douglas Day Stewart (*An Officer and a Gentleman*). Stewart Stern (*Rebel Without a Cause*) developed my senior thesis screenplay. I had one professor who let each of my classmates hold his best original screenplay Oscar after he read our senior thesis treatments and declared, "None of you will ever touch one again." He resigned the next day to write a script in Dublin about James Joyce. The teacher who replaced him was this TV writer none of us had ever heard of and we were like, "What are your credits?" This substitute professor, who'd taught screenwriting to death row inmates, told us she'd written countless episodes of *Three's Company*, which impressed the hell out of us. But my favorite was the Filmic Writing 101 professor who gave everyone in the class a red-inked F after we turned in our very first writing assignment.

Dollars: Sounds like a dick move. Why did he give you an F?

Mersault: He said he wanted us to get used to rejection.

Dollars: Everything I picked up I learned from my neighbor who wrote the Clint Eastwood orangutan movies. Wasn't there a baseball script you wrote that Ron Howard wanted to direct when you were just a freshman?

Mersault: You're talking about *Fowl Ball*, which started out as a twenty-two page treatment written by the *Washington Post* sportswriter Tony Kornheiser about a Baltimore Orioles pitcher and a catcher, a battery, who decide to play one last season for the worst team in the Mexican League, the Juarez Pollos.

Dollars: Was there a bidding war? How much did Brian pay for the script?

Mersault: I never met Brian Grazer or Ron Howard. One of the bits of advice I got from my Dad was to get the rights to this baseball story Tony Kornheiser had written before I went to film school. I met with Tony and convinced him to give me the rights to *Fowl Ball* in exchange for fifty percent of whatever proceeds I got from the sale of the screenplay. Tony decided that fifty percent of something was better than a hundred percent of nothing and signed over the rights. A few months later, when I came home for Christmas break, I was sleeping in and my mom started screaming from downstairs that Ron Howard was calling from Century City. I was half asleep and thought she was just saying that Ron Howard stuff to get me to start my day. I woke up and found this note with an unfamiliar name and a phone number to call Imagine

Films about *Fowl Ball.* I got on the phone with Imagine Films VP Michael Billingsley and he told me he used to be an assistant at CAA where he read this treatment called *Fowl Ball* by Tony Kornheiser that Tom Hanks wanted to do with Peter Scolari, his costar from *Bosom Buddies,* that ABC sitcom where two guys pretend to be women in order to live in a cheap all-women's apartment building. Michael said he reached out to Kornheiser and asked him what ever happened to *Fowl Ball* and Tony said, "Talk to Mersault. He's got the rights." I told Michael I was coming back to LA for film school and that I would be happy to meet him. But there was no script yet. I hadn't sat down and fleshed out the treatment or even written *Fade In.* I had a classmate who was a standup comedian and wrote jokes for comics who worked every night at The Comedy Store, so I suggested we write the script together. Michael Billingsley said when *Fowl Ball* was ready he would show it to Ron Howard for Tom Hanks and Peter Scolari. We wrote the first draft for free and turned it into Imagine, expecting this enormous check. Instead we got a five-page creative memo on Imagine stationary. We executed the notes, turned in a second draft, waited for the check. Then there was a writer's strike in nineteen eighty-eight and we put our pencils down and wore WGA solidarity T-shirts on campus even though we weren't Guild members. We didn't hear from Michael Billingsley for a couple of weeks until he called to say he'd left Imagine Films to take a development job at Paramount for the producer of the *Friday the 13th* movies and we would have story meetings in Michael's office with a cardboard lobby statue of Jason Voorhees waving a machete over our heads. Paramount passed on our script and that was it. *Fowl Ball* was dead. The last time I saw Michael Billingsley I gave him a novel I'd found called *The Player* because he reminded me of Michael Tolkin's studio executive.

Dollars: Did the failure to sell *Fowl Ball* sour you on the business or were you hooked now that you'd had a taste of driving on the Paramount lot as a screenwriter?

Mersault: It made me hungrier. I ordered a California vanity license plate that said SCRWRTER. Eventually I had to change my plates because people would roll down their car windows at red lights to ask me if I wrote porn films.

Dollars: Your classmates must have been jealous about Ron Howard?

Mersault: Probably, but they got really envious when John Singleton made a deal to direct his senior thesis script *Boyz N The Hood* for Columbia Pictures and came to class with a red CAA script cover. I went to class with black Omniscience script covers because I was reading for them.

Dollars: How did you get that gig at Omniscience?

Mersault: This young agent came to speak at our class and told us he started as a reader because, "Screenplays are the currency of the business." My classmates were dismissive: "God, I hope I'm not a reader when I get out of here." I went up to the Omniscience agent afterward and asked him how does someone become a script reader? To his eternal credit, he told me to drop his name with the head of the story department at Omniscience and see if that got me an interview. I may have stretched the truth when I told the story department the agent was my cousin. That got me a test script to cover called *The Rookie*, which I liked for Charlie Sheen, who ended up making it with Clint Eastwood. The story department asked me to review another script called *The Hard Way* for director John Badham, who got the job after I gave the script a recommend. I liked another script called *Midnight Run* for Charles Grodin to play the accountant. They officially hired me when Clint Eastwood's agent appreciated what I said about *The Rookie* and requested me specifically to be Charlie Sheen's personal script reader. Now, at thirty-five bucks a coverage, I couldn't live on what they were paying me, so I took a side job driving prostitutes around in Hollywood. The job began at midnight and I would pick up these two girls, Daisy James and her roommate Cricket, whose boyfriend Terrondus was in prison and used to be their driver. They didn't own a car so I got paid a hundred bucks a show to take them wherever they had to go. The deal was, I would walk them up to the client's house as the muscle, take the cash donation, or use the credit card machine, and wait an hour in the car until they emerged from the front door. I would put the top down on my Chrysler convertible and drive under a street lamp, read scripts, and write the coverage by hand. This became a habit of mine: to write down my thoughts on the back of every script. As their beck and call driver, Daisy and Cricket would feed me at Sushi on Sunset and pay for my gas. Sometimes they would get jobs for a topless scene in some Erik Estrada straight-to-video movie and I would get paid to drive them to the set or they'd pay me twenty bucks to drive them to Rock and Roll Ralphs on Sunset so they could go grocery shopping. I was making good money driving them around a couple nights a week, two shows a night at a hundred bucks a pop. Sometimes I made more when I drove them to bachelor parties and they would share the tips with their driver. Sometimes the job meant putting my life at risk, but it was cash money, enough to cover the rent, and I really liked working for those scary pimps in the Valley. At Omniscience, my life was never in danger, but I had to be Machiavellian to get noticed by the agents. I would ask the story department if I could drop off my scripts and coverage directly to the motion picture agents on the second floor at Omniscience. John Cusack's agent was on the phone when I delivered my coverage to her office and she said, "Excuse me, who are you?" and when I told the agent my name, she said Cusack wanted me exclusively to evaluate every piece of material submitted for him. When Cusack came to Omniscience for a meet and greet with all the agents in the motion picture department, Cusack's agent insisted I attend the meeting. I told her I couldn't go because I was a freelance reader and not an agency employee and she said, "That doesn't help me." Next thing I knew I was promoted to in-house staff reader with a salary, an office, a couch, a computer, no assistant, minimum of ten scripts a week. In the Cusack meeting I sat in the back while agents pitched him projects and every time a script was raised Cusack would look across the room for my reaction. Agents caught on, and for the next couple weeks I never got so many compliments in my life.

Dollars: Did Cusack ever do anything nice for you?

Mersault: One night I was at a bar called the Lava Lounge with my best friend and we were about to leave with these drunk stewardesses and one of them looked behind me and said, "Oh my god, it's John Cusack." And I said, "Really, where?" Cusack waved us over and bought a round of Heinekens. The stewardesses did not go home with us.

Dollars: What happened to driving Miss Daisy?

Mersault: The last time I saw Daisy James, she gave me the novel *Leaving Laughlin* as a goodbye present. I told the scary pimps in the Valley they needed a new driver.

Dollars: Did the pimps in Beverly Hills give you a nice office?

Mersault: I wasn't used to an office environment, so in the beginning I would take my scripts and read them by the pool at the Beverly Wilshire Hotel. When I was done, I'd toss them in the water: the good ones would float, and if they sunk, they stunk. One afternoon I got really sunburned and ditched the chaise lounge for my windowless office on El Habanero Drive.

LEAVING LAUGHLIN
Screenplay by Ben Sanderson

COMMENTS: Bleak, dark, dramatic material that's strangely life-affirming and compelling. Essentially a two-character piece with Laughlin, Nevada in the background, story revolves around PALE, a terrible alcoholic who comes to Laughlin to drink himself to death only to be temporarily saved by NIKKI, a prostitute who's living a death wish, too. They turn a trick into a brief relationship that's at times romantic, grim, and devastating. Script is often explicit in its no-holds-barred depiction of alcoholism and prostitution. That is part of its bitter charm. The characters Pale and Nikki are well-drawn, equals in misery and made for each other. Her life on the streets is as harrowing as his obsession with the bottle. Dialogue is spare, but loaded and honest. Gritty tale about a hooker who wants to save the john is true to its memorable source material (novel by John O'Brien) and might be too dark for the masses but with the right casting this could expand its target audience.

Dollars: So, who died and made you the head of the story department?

Mersault: Nobody died. What happened was, there was this exodus of agents leaving the motion picture department over money and the culture and they were almost all women: Ronnie Almond, Janine Joy, Marlene Mounds, and Annette Raisin. I heard this story how Ronnie Almond bolted from Omniscience after she was mistakenly handed a year-end bonus check for a male agent also named Ronnie that dwarfed what she had ever received from the company. Clients flew out the door to follow their agents down the street to rival agency Insanely Creative Artists. Then, Abbadon happened.

Dollars: That was the nineteen ninety-two Omniscience acquisition of boutique agency Abbadon, led by über-übers Lester Barnes and Arthur Zagnut for their music acts and motion picture client lists.

Mersault: The timing of my promotion as staff reader was exquisite. Lester Barnes represented DQ, one of the biggest movie stars in the world. Zagnut represented John Travolta, Patrick Swayze, and Whitney Houston. The music department had a license to print money, representing Nirvana and Pearl Jam and Perry Farrell's Lollapalooza. Our new worldwide head of the motion picture department, Lester Barnes, needed a reader and that became my job. Every script I read for DQ typically began with the character described as ruggedly handsome and every other script I read was a *Die Hard* knockoff: *Die Hard* on a date, *Die Hard* at the Post Office, *Die Hard* in a closet (that one was called *Coat Hanger*). There was even a script at Warner Brothers that was *Die Hard* in a skyscraper. I read *The Rock*, but not for DQ. I forget who I read it for, maybe Sam Elliott.

Dollars: If you only read garbage, how come you didn't leave Omniscience?

Mersault: I didn't read garbage every day, I read cream. Being the in-house staff reader for Omniscience meant I mostly evaluated studio pictures and firm offers. Then the head of the story department resigned and I was the only one in the building running the place while the agency interviewed outside candidates to become the new department head. For a week I was assigning overnight coverage and acting like the boss to all the outside readers. The assistant I inherited told me to go across the street for a meeting with the head of business affairs and the head of the motion picture literary department. I called my dad first to tell him they were probably going to offer me the position as head of the story department, and ask him, if they did offer the job, should I take it? Dad said, "Son, up is up." So I went to the office of the literary department honcho and the agent said, "Look, this job will drive you crazy. You're going to have to hire and fire people, manage the agent trainees, and still write coverage yourself." The head lawyer said, "You don't want this job. We know you write scripts. Maybe one day the agency will represent you." I asked them if they were offering me the job and they said, "Yes." I said, very fast: "ThankyouverymuchIaccept," and ran out of that office. Up was up.

TEA IN THE SAHARA
Screenplay by Samantha Strong

COMMENTS: Well-written historical drama painted on a large canvas with memorable characters caught in a tragic love story that turns out to be as involving as a mystery. Set during WWII, at a villa that's been converted into a hospital, a badly burned patient is brought to the care of emotionally fragile nurse NANA. Through well-constructed flashbacks, we learn about the emotionally-packed love story of PIERRE and the married AIMEE during an international expedition in nineteen thirty-nine North Africa. When their affair is discovered, Aimee's husband tries to kill them all with his plane, but he only kills himself and wounds Aimee. Tragically, when Pierre is forced to leave Aimee in a cave while he goes for help, he is captured by soldiers who suspect him to be German and Aimee is dead by the time he returns to the cave. Under Nana's care, Pierre encourages her to help him commit suicide. Richly realized script smartly offers strong subplots that add narrative and emotional layers: the angry Intelligence officer PISTACHIO, maimed by the Germans, suspects Pierre is a Nazi spy and debates killing him; Nana herself is given a heartbroken past (through flashbacks) and a light romance with an Indian, VINDALOO, that touches on interracial dynamics. Sometimes it feels like there's too much going on here, and the question of whether Pierre is a spy or not doesn't play as important as the Pierre-Aimee love story. There's a lot to resolve here, fortunately this material succeeds in spinning a gripping, romantic tale. Dialogue is excellent, intelligent, thoughtful. Characterizations are well-drawn, layered, distinct; each role could be either a showcase turn or memorable support. With its leisurely pacing, nonlinear structure, and subtle character, this feels slightly against the mainstream grain. But it is a love story that works on a universal level that resonates with a powerful chord. It's a strong narrative, well told, with stunning desert vistas that make this material special and deserving of our attention.

BOX OF CHOCOLATES
Screenplay by Louis Broth

COMMENTS: Winning, amusing comedy with fantasy elements about MILTON QWIRTZ, a mentally challenged man who relates his rather incredible, illustrious, and fulfilling life experiences to perfect strangers at a bus stop. Not unlike Chauncey Gardner in BEING THERE, Milton's life is filled with misunderstandings and fortuitous events. As the script covers the fifties, sixties, seventies, and eighties, Milton has memorable encounters with famous real people such as ELVIS, KENNEDY, MARTIN LUTHER KING, CHAIRMAN MAO, the BLACK PANTHERS, the WATERGATE BURGLARS, and NIXON. Script also successfully employs, without overdoing it, Milton's unusual point of view in which surreal visions occasionally appear. Simply told, the script unfolds through flashbacks and while this back-and-forth structure occasionally feels awkward, still manages to make this overused narrative device work. Packed with memorable moments, strong dialogue, and a signature role for DQ, this is a completely character-driven story of a life lived well.

I HEART SHAKESPEARE
Screenplay by Alexander Dobreanu

EVALUATION: This is a charming, romantic script about Shakespeare and the woman who broke his heart. WILL SHAKESPEARE starts a new play, ROMEO & JULIET, as a comedy. But when he falls in love with LINDA DE BESSUPS, a lady in waiting whose hand has been given to a scoundrel named ESSEX, Will finds himself, and his play, changing for the better. Linda agrees to marry Essex only after he threatens to shut down Will's theatre. Inspired by his pain and heartbreak, ROMEO & JULIET becomes a tragedy. The concept is brilliant and supported by a first-rate execution. The Elizabethan dialogue works well, accompanied by the sheer poetry of Shakespeare's own words. Characters are rich and believable. This well-written screenplay should appeal to directors, stars, and audiences alike. Unabashedly romantic, funny, and dramatic, the Bard himself would appreciate this lovestruck fantasy.

Dollars: Running the Omniscience story department sounds like this amazing job where you can take a script and do anything, with this incredible access to agents, movie stars, producers, and directors.

Mersault: You have to be judicious with that access. I didn't really know how much goodwill I actually had inside the motion picture department until I fell in love with this script called *The Grey Area* written by a director client named Franklin Brauner and his wife. Their agent told me to call them after I'd read it and take them out to lunch. I hit the couch, closed the door, and finished reading their script in one sitting, always a good sign. I didn't need to throw this script into the pool to see if it would float or sink. I knew I had gold. When I told this older agent I was meeting the director Franklin Brauner, he snorted contemptuously and asked if I'd been to his house in the hills yet? His knowing wink suggested I could expect to take part in an unwanted orgy. I rented Franklin Brauner's movies so I could be familiar with his work before we met. His last produced credit was this nineteen eighty-nine cult movie *White of the Eye* that got a limited theatrical release.

In the seventies, Franklin Brauner directed this trippy, Kubrickian science-fiction movie called *Demon Seed* with Julie Christie trapped in her automated house controlled by an artificially intelligent computer who impregnates her to create a diabolical offspring. Then I watched Franklin Brauner's debut film *Performance*, starring Mick Jagger, a hallucinatory film made in the late sixties that played like two movies: The first half was a British gangster film about a mob enforcer that seemed to be the inspiration for *Reservoir Dogs* with its funny criminal talk and explosive violence. The second half was a drug-fueled romp in a London flat owned by a reclusive rock star, where the gangster lays low from a contract put out on his life. Jagger played a version of himself, a libertine named Turner with two concubines doing him and magic mushrooms all day and all night. There was a line from Mick Jagger in the movie that perfectly described Franklin Brauner's filmography: "The only performance that makes it, that really makes it all the way, is madness." So, having prepped for my meeting with Franklin Brauner and his wife, our lunch was a love fest and they invited me afterwards to go to the movies with them and I think we saw Kieślowski's *Blue* together, followed by an invitation to dinner at Café Des Artistes because they needed a fourth to join them. When I sat down at their table, Mick Jagger, wearing a purple sweater, asked me to pass the bread basket. Eventually, I struck up a conversation with Mick regarding my uncle's historical novel about the famous hypnotist Anton Mesmer because I remembered his movie company Jagged Films once inquired about the film rights. Mick suggested they adapt the book for Franklin to direct. The next day, when I told my mom I had dinner with Mick Jagger, there was this pause, and she said, "Yeah right, and tomorrow you're having breakfast with Keith Richards."

THE GREY AREA
Screenplay by Franklin Brauner & Asia King

COMMENTS: Erotic, dark thriller with razor-sharp characters thrust into bent situations that force them to reexamine their lives. Heavily in debt, bank official LULU LOPEZ moonlights as a high-class call girl and becomes involved with charismatic money launderer, BRUNO BIRMINGHAM, whose chauffeur, MAXWELL, is an undercover Justice Department agent out to nab his boss. The unexpected happens when Lulu has a cathartic sexual awakening with Bruno's lesbian ex-wife, CAROLINA CHOW, who unleashes Lulu's inhibitions, and unravels Maxwell's carefully planned sting operation. Script handles the money laundering details with a plausible, intriguing computer scam involving a "Hiroshima" virus that will cover Bruno's tracks. Behind the numbers game are deliciously drawn characters that resonate with their unique brand of intelligence, attitude, and risky business. Bruno Birmingham is charismatic and kinky, a brilliant money launderer who charges thirteen percent to wash dirty money. Lulu is enchanting and reckless, a dynamic female lead who undergoes a spirited sexual awakening. Justice Department agent Maxwell is tough, cocky, and potentially memorable. Dialogue is the muscle of the piece, chewy and explicit, with a wicked sense of humor. For those who like sex, money, and danger (in no particular order), script's deeply drawn characters are the real stars of this sexy material.

Dollars: Was there a trigger that brought the financing? How did you work internally to package this material and ultimately get it made?

Mersault: The first thing Franklin Brauner asked me was, "Did I know the agent for Christopher Walken so he could play Bruno?" I said I would get Walken to read *The Grey Area*. I went to the agent's office, threw my coverage on his desk, and declared this was "a great script" by Franklin Brauner and that he should send it to Christopher Walken. At first the agent only wanted to know if I'd ever been up to Franklin Brauner's house in the Hollywood Hills. He seemed hesitant to send the script because Franklin Brauner was attached to direct but my passion for the material won the day. A few weeks later, Franklin Brauner called to say they were having drinks with Christopher Walken at the Chateau Marmont because the star was obsessed with the script, introducing himself as Bruno Birmingham on the phone with them. Their first meeting went well and Christopher Walken attached himself to the project. Franklin Brauner then asked me if I could get Joan Chen to play Bruno's ex-wife. I said I would attach Joan Chen to the project. On the second floor of Omniscience, Franklin Brauner's agent went to visit Joan Chen's agent and asked if Joan would consider playing a lesbian in a Franklin Brauner movie and the agent said he just had lunch with Joan Chen and she told him to find her a movie where she could portray a lesbian. Next they wanted Steven Bauer from *Scarface* to play Maxwell the chauffeur and a few weeks after I gave their script to his agent they met with Steven Bauer and found their Maxwell. I had created my first Omniscience package with a cast that was totally committed to the script and supportive of their enigmatic director. Franklin Brauner's agent found a financier to put up the money and a start date was announced at the Cannes Film Festival. Now, the only role in the script that remained open was the female lead, which Franklin Brauner and the producers fought over every day during preproduction. Anne Heche was cast as the bisexual banker and a year later at the Oscars she fell in love with Ellen DeGeneres and they became the most famous lesbians on the planet. I thought Heche was still in character from *The Grey Area*. I finally got invited to Franklin Brauner's house in the Hollywood Hills at the very top of Sunset Plaza Drive and I realized why every agent would ask me about going up there: It was the most spectacular view of Los Angeles I'd ever seen.

Dollars: I watched *The Grey Area*. You're pretty good in those scenes opposite Steven Bauer and Anne Heche. Tell us how you got cast and what happened with the finished film?

Mersault: Franklin wrote a small part for me to play as a thank you to the reader who put their movie together. I got along famously with Anne Heche when we practiced our lines together in the hair and makeup trailer before filming. I had this one scene with Steven Bauer where he went off script and started ad-libbing. I didn't have that skill set so I would freeze up every time I tried to improvise something clever. I'm sure I was terrible in every one of my scenes, but after a screening at Omniscience this agent thought I was so brilliant she wanted to put me up for a part in Michael Mann's *Heat* as one of the guys in De Niro's crew.

Dollars: Tell me you went to the audition at Warner Brothers.

Mersault: I didn't, the part ended up going to Henry Rollins. The morning of my big scene with

Anne Heche and Steven Bauer I thought I was having a heart attack. Driving to the set of *The Grey Area* on the PCH, I started losing feeling in my hands. I couldn't catch my breath. I pulled over at a gas station and called nine-one-one with numb fingers. A fire truck and ambulance arrived in five minutes. The paramedic, who looked like Ashley Judd, took my pulse and asked me where was I going? I informed her I was an actor going to a movie set in Malibu. She said my vitals were fine, probably just a panic attack. I thanked her for saving my life and went to the set. This bearded grip came up to me and said he saw me at a gas station surrounded by an ambulance and a paramedic taking my pulse. I denied it was me three times but that grip pretty much told everyone on set I had freaked out. I read scripts for Omniscience all day in my trailer until I did my one scene. I was driving home on the PCH when I started losing feeling in my hands. I pulled into this Mexican place and ordered a burrito when I heard someone ask me, "Where were you? I went to your set today." I turned around and it was the Ashley Judd paramedic. I told her I must have been in my trailer. Then she said there was an accident on the set, a fake phone booth had fallen on a grip and separated his shoulder. I prayed to the movie gods it was my Judas grip that had looked up at the falling phone booth. For the second time that day, her angelic presence made the panic attack disappear. My burrito arrived, I winked at the paramedic, and she said, "You know how to reach me, just call nine-one-one."

Dollars: So what happened to *The Grey Area*, did it play the festivals and get picked up by Harvey Weinstein?

Mersault: After Franklin Brauner turned in his first cut, the producers locked him out of the editing room and hired the editors from the TV show *Cops* to ruin his masterpiece, leave Christopher Walken's career-best turn on the cutting room floor, and transform *The Grey Area* into an atrocity. Since it was no longer his film, Franklin took his name off the picture. Instead of screening Franklin Brauner's cut for Harvey Weinstein, the producers sold *The Grey Area* to HBO. I was jaywalking across El Habanero Drive when an agent told me Franklin Brauner killed himself. At his memorial service I spoke about the last time I saw Franklin alive, eating huevos rancheros at Duke's Coffee Shop on

Sunset, yellow cheese stuck on his goateed chin, the director talking animatedly about his next picture. Years after his death, his widow got a UK distributor for the director's cut. I had to pick myself off the floor and do it all over again, servicing agents and their clients with scripts. I snapped out of that funk when I got called in to a meeting with Jennifer Love Hewitt who needed a great script to launch her new production company, Love Spell Entertainment, at Sony. I suggested a script that was in turnaround at United Artists about a young woman haunted by the surfing accident that claimed the life of her brother and she takes up surfing to find out what happened to him and ends up finding out who she really is. Next thing I knew, that script *Girl in the Curl* was announced as the first Sony project for Love Spell Entertainment. What happened was: she read the script.

Dollars: I know that awful feeling of picking yourself off the floor. Grief brought me to Los Angeles. My girlfriend Cybelle was murdered by a serial killer who found his victims through the classifieds.

Mersault: Dollars, you don't have to go–

Dollars: Cybelle was working for this music video director and she was selling his Avid editing equipment for him and she got a call from this guy who agreed to her price and told her to drive the Avid over to his place. Cybelle asked me to help her carry the equipment. The guy changed his address on us twice and we almost didn't go through with it but her boss was in a hurry to get rid of the editing equipment so she agreed to meet him at this motel near LaGuardia. I was carrying the Avid stuff inside when the guy closed the door and the last thing I saw was him swinging this hammer at my head. I went to the hospital with a skull fracture and not much chance to survive. He didn't even take the Avid. I missed Cybelle's funeral because I was in a medically-induced coma. A year later I was still a wreck when I got a phone call from this reality TV producer inviting me to catch the Klassifieds Killer on their show *Wanted: Dead or Alive* by helping them stage the dramatic recreation of Cybelle's murder. They put me up at a hotel across the street from CBS, and when I got to the production office they brought me in to casting sessions and gave me a nametag that said "Victim." They cast this girl who looked so much like Cybelle I avoided her during the shoot. I actually ended up hanging out the most with the actor playing Cybelle's killer.

Mersault: They never caught the guy?

Dollars: The episode aired, nothing happened. Instead of going back east, I stayed in Los Angeles and rented a guest house where I started writing, got an agent, and sold my first script to Savoy Pictures, *Alive and Kicking*, about a guy who avenges his girlfriend's murder when he participates in a crime solvers program and realizes the killer is the TV host who invited him on the show.

WHAT'S THE SECRET TO WRITING A REALLY SMART EVALUATION?

Mersault: Say everything you want to say about the material in the first sentence. Describe the script's execution with the very first word (exhilarating, hilarious, uneven). Have an attitude that every agent or client reading your coverage is probably multitasking, either on the phone, getting a manicure or a blowjob, on a treadmill, or texting someone while glancing at your coverage, and they are only going to read the opening kicker sentence and see if it got a recommend or a pass. Your job is to describe the script, starting with the premise. How is it executed? Does it consistently engage you? Is the script populated with dimensional and castable characters? How is the dialogue? Describe the talk. What is the tone of the piece? Define it. Reference another movie. When you have run out of things to say about a script, you're done. People who dismiss readers as thoughtless executioners fail to appreciate the flip side to that coin: Anybody who's about to write coverage wants to have their socks knocked off, and when they have gold in their hands they want to promote the hell out of that script because that's what the business runs on: passion and material.

I WORK AT WHOLE FOODS. HOW DO I GET AN AGENT?

Mersault: Omniscience once asked me to speak at Career Day at Crenshaw, an inner-city high school with metal detectors and security guards. The principal called me the night before to make sure I was still coming, I told him to expect me at eight o'clock sharp on the school grounds and I jokingly said I wanted a Crenshaw Football T-shirt as my payment for speaking. Next morning the principal greeted me with a Crenshaw Football T-shirt and an ROTC military escort for my first class at Career Day. The students in the classroom were indifferent until I told them I once played a crack dealer as an extra in John Singleton's *Boyz N The Hood.* Then they asked me, "How much money do you make?" and "What kind of car do you drive?" In my last class of the day, this tall varsity football player named Antwone said if I wore that Crenshaw T-shirt in his neighborhood people would look at me funny. I invited Antwone to my neighborhood, promised him an Omniscience T-shirt, and said if people in Beverly Hills saw him wearing that shirt they would think he was a client. The class laughed. Antwone thought they were laughing at him and told me to stop playing with him. I walked over and gave Antwone my business card and told him to come by the office next week anytime. A week later: no word from Antwone. We had an Omniscience T-shirt and baseball cap ready for the kid, but he never showed up. The principal of Crenshaw called me a couple months later and my first thought was Antwone got murdered, but the principal wasn't calling about Antwone. He said his son was an aspiring screenwriter in San Diego and could he call me for some career advice? I said of course and hung up the phone. Thirty seconds later, my phone rang and it was the son of the principal, all nervous and grateful to be speaking with

"Mr. Mersault." I said, "Mr. Mersault is my father. Call me Larry." Son of the principal told me his day job was selling Padres season tickets over the phone, and while he liked the steady paycheck his real passion was writing. I asked him how many scripts he'd written. He said, "Five." I asked him to tell me the premise of his latest screenplay and he said it was about an Islamic exorcism of a female US soldier in Jalalabad. I told him to e-mail me the script with no expectations that anything would happen. I read it, loved it, gave the script to this Icelandic director client who read it, loved it, gave *The Exorcism of Private Slovik* to his agent, who signed the writer and set it up at Paramount Insurge with Michael Bay producing. Dollars, stop texting while I'm talking!

WHAT HAPPENED TO ANTWONE?

Mersault: Antwone was a beast for USC. He got drafted in the second round by the Seattle Seahawks.

I KNOW WHO KILLED CYBELLE

Mersault: That's not funny.

Dollars: Can you tell us anything specific about that day?

SHE HAD BREAST REDUCTION SURGERY

Dollars: And how the fuck do you know that?

I LICKED THOSE SCARS

Dollars: Of course you did. After you killed her.

Mersault: Dollars, we can stop now. This is sick–

Dollars: Let's keep that guy talking. You good for another hour?

Mersault: I'm here until you say it's over.

Dollars: You're twenty-five years old when they make you the head of the story department, that's a lot of power.

Mersault: I wouldn't exactly call the position powerful. Ultimately, the client decides, not the reader, which script they make. The story department was, at best, a filter, a moat around the castle to protect royalty from the barbarians storming the gate. I took reading scripts very seriously and it became my life's work. I didn't see my perch as a stepping stone to do something else, like go work for a studio or a production company, I wanted to do something extraordinary with the story department at Omniscience. I'm sorry, what was the question again?

Dollars: I forgot. You described the story department as a moat, a line of defense against bad scripts. Who were the readers you hired and how could you trust them?

Mersault: Someone once said if you only hire people smaller than you are, you will have a company of dwarves. If you work with people bigger than you are, you will have a company of giants. I wanted to create a Murderer's Row of readers like the nineteen twenty-seven New York Yankees. I sought out experienced readers who spoke the language to break down material for agents and their clients. If I thought you were smarter than me, I hired you.

Dollars: What do you mean "speak the language"?

Mersault: I wanted readers who could speak the industry lingo so confidently and effortlessly that agents would instantly trust their judgment. You had to be able to praise or dismiss what you'd read with a knowing reference, an insider's attitude about material. I liked hiring writer's assistants, Scott Rudin refugees, and out of work outliers, loaded with industry experience, like a producer on the lot who lost her housekeeping deal or an unemployed reader with five thousand scripts under his belt now taking care of a parent with Alzheimer's. I would interview people on Thursday morning and give them a test script with the title page ripped off, which I called Script A, so they didn't know what they were reading. If you passed on Script A, I didn't hire you, something was wrong with you, and believe me, a lot of people passed. If you didn't pass on this script I would look at what you had to say about the screenplay's voice and viability. I couldn't use Script A for very long because Gus Van Sant signed on to direct and the movie would go on to win the Oscar for best original screenplay. Ultimately, Script A was a terrific inkblot and the applicants I hired turned out to be very, very good readers for Omniscience.

SCRIPT A

Screenplay by N/A

COMMENTS: Excellent dramatic piece that packs the emotional kick of ORDINARY PEOPLE with a believable, down to earth yarn that may not offer the most commercial storyline, yet delivers an outstanding execution through its completely character-driven narrative. Cal Tech janitor PACO RUNYON runs with a rough Arab crowd of guys he considers his family when he's arrested for fighting. Cal Tech professor JANETTI gets him out of trouble when he realizes Paco is a math genius. As part of the plea bargain, Paco undergoes counseling with shrink MEHRING, an old friend of Janetti's, who's struggling with the death of his wife to cancer. Paco talks about his abuse as an orphan and eventually comes to terms with his issues of abandonment. Mehring and Janetti are also affected by this young man and they grow as a result of the experience. Script offers a believable, compelling romance between Paco and blind masseuse TEAL, who's much more than just a pretty peach, but a woman who helps Paco break down his walls. Technically, script is superb: dialogue-heavy, but the talk is funny, natural, and memorable.

Characters are crisp and weighty: Janetti and Mehring are distinct and well-drawn, sure to interest older actors who'd like to try them on for size. Ending with Paco and his therapist getting down to a conclusion about each other is moving as hell. For our director clients, brave material could be memorable and end up touching a lot of people.

Dollars: Tell me, what is the Sundance Film Festival like?

Mersault: I've only been once. I came home from work and my roommate held up this VHS tape and asked me if I wanted to see a real, honest-to-god snuff film. So we watched this raw video footage, no opening credits, just this obnoxious film student named Heather ordering around these two dudes with cameras and they're getting ready to go on this trip–

Dollars: Sounds like *The Blair Witch Project.*

Mersault: I'm watching this fucking scary movie and I kept saying to my roommate, "Oh man, this is bullshit, this ain't real, wait, is it?" And then they find that house at the end, those handprints on the walls, and the camera goes dead. I hadn't been that scared since I snuck into the Uptown Theatre when I was twelve to watch *The Shining*. I took the VHS tape to our independent film division and insisted they represent this handheld horror movie at Sundance.

Dollars: Of course you did. How much did they get for it?

Mersault: They passed. Too many handheld shots of leaves, they said. Years later the movie gods came back with a shot at redemption. There was a screening at Omniscience of a no-budget horror movie looking for representation called *The Gainesville Evidence.* I was the only one inside the Aidikoff theatre and they didn't cancel the screening. I motioned to the projectionist to run the picture and I watched *The Gainesville Evidence* by myself. I couldn't believe it was happening again, that indescribable feeling of discovery, like the time Dad and I screened *Reservoir Dogs*. An agent walked into the Aidikoff and asked if the picture was any good and I told the agent he had to represent this fucking classic or I would sell it myself at Park City. A month later I woke up at four in the morning in the Omniscience condo to find a text from that agent: "Just sold *Gainesville Evidence* for two million. You are my horror maven." Then I had breakfast with Bob Tanner, Dad's best friend from the Marine Corps, the guy who got me into USC Film School, who was retired and lived in Park City. I told Tanner how happy I was to see him at Sundance, how much I enjoyed working at Omniscience and he was smiling the whole time, bursting with pride. The check arrived for our breakfast and I grabbed it off the table and told him, "Bob, let me get this."

THAT'S IT? A DENVER OMELETTE FOR CHANGING YOUR LIFE?

Dollars: Nobody asked you for your opinion.

SHOOT THE DOG
Screenplay by Manley Halliday

COMMENTS: Strangelove for the nineties. Wonderfully subversive, well-written black comedy packs an intriguing combination of combat movie, Hollywood story, and political drama. Plot is reminiscent of CAPRICORN ONE (which postulated a fake moon landing) with the President and his advisors creating a hoax war with Brazil over sugar cane fields in order to ensure the President's reelection. Out of work screenwriter DUDLEY DRAISH gets the assignment to concoct the build-up, the tension, the speeches, the soldiers' heroism, patriotic flourishes, and a climactic battle sequence. Dudley discovers, to his horror, that he's not writing a movie but a real war broadcast nightly on CNN. There's a risk when the script plays so inside Hollywood, but somehow this pulls off its hugely ambitious concept and makes a brilliant satire on war movies ("Ain't Gonna Bury Me!"), Hollywood types ("Heard you were in Rehab"), and a timely political drama with all the nuances of a White House drama. Script is undeniably filmic with its self-reflexivity and multimedia presentation

(TVs, commercials, film, video, and script pages). For DQ, heroic screenwriter Dudley, painted with cynical brushstrokes, is definitely worth considering. Supporting characters are ruthless Washington types and venal movie people who could be Siamese twins so alike are they in nature, goals, and personalities. Combining elements of CAPRICORN ONE, THE PLAYER, and NO WAY OUT, this has to go for broke with star casting and a visionary director to pull it off.

WHAT'S THE FASTEST COVERAGE YOU EVER WROTE?

Mersault: I once got a script at noon and this agent needed a report before his lunch with Drew Barrymore. There was no way it could be done, so of course I accepted the assignment. I only read the dialogue. It was the story of *Boys Don't Cry*, not the one that got made, but this other, competing Brandon Teena project. The story was fairly linear and easy to summarize. I read the script in half an hour, wrote the logline in sixty seconds, the summary and evaluation as fast as I could, and e-mailed it off at twelve-fifty to the agent's office. I was kind of disappointed when I didn't get a brownie basket. For my efforts working on the *Norbit* script, Eddie Murphy's people sent me this obscene champagne and fruit basket that fed every reader who came by to pick up scripts and we drained that magnum all day. I worked with Wes Craven once and the master of horror sent me a thank you bottle of wine that was so velvety I thought I was drinking blood.

WHO'S THE BIGGEST STAR AT OMNISCIENCE YOU EVER READ FOR?

Mersault: Omniscience signed Hugo Slater after his last movie, *Break the Bank,* didn't at the box office and his agents invited me to join the team. Soon, Hugo Slater was calling me "Reader Guy," as in, "What does Reader Guy say about the script?" I felt this awesome responsibility to contribute to his legacy of films and the first script I thought was worthy was *I Am Legend* at Warner Brothers. The studio attached Hugo Slater to star and then Ridley Scott came on board to direct with a hundred-million-dollar budget.

Dollars: A hundred million nowadays is a bargain. What happened? When *I Am Legend* came out, Will Smith was fighting the vampires.

Mersault: I forget what year it was, but there were several projects that Warner Brothers decided ultimately not to make. It came down to *I Am Legend*, a reboot of *Superman* with Tim Burton, and a Renny Harlin shark movie called *Deep Blue Sea*. The movie gods did not smile on Hugo Slater. The studio chose the shark movie. *I Am Legend* became *I Am Not Happening* and I had to read all these scripts for Hugo Slater to find his next picture. One of them was called *Man's Fate* by Michael Cimino, based on the novel by André Malreaux, and I passed on it, but Hugo's agent asked me to take the director out to lunch, listen to Cimino tell me a few stories, pay the check, and break it to him that Hugo Slater wasn't interested in *Man's Fate*. I arrived at Café Roma in Beverly Hills for my Michael Cimino lunch with a package that had the director's name scrawled on it. At our table, Cimino unwrapped the gift and found a small wooden coffin that slid open, revealing a photograph of Michael Cimino with two Oscars for *The Deer Hunter*. Cimino was so stunned by the handcarved coffin he looked at me and said, "Who are you?" Lunch became this memory lane about writing the screenplay with William Peter Blatty, who wrote *The Exorcist*, and how determined Cimino was to make *Handcarved Coffins* after *Man's Fate*. I paid the bill and delicately informed Cimino that Hugo Slater wasn't going to star in his script. Cimino took the news well. He held up his handcarved coffin and said, "That's okay, I have this."

Dollars: Sylvester Stallone was originally going to star in *Beverly Hills Cop*. I'm interested in hearing what were some of the scripts you championed that, for whatever reason, Hugo Slater didn't make?

Mersault: I walked into our weekly Hugo Slater meeting humming the theme song from the seventies TV show *S.W.A.T.* and that's how Hugo Slater got attached to play Hondo, the leader of this elite squad escorting an international criminal to his sentencing hearing with every bad guy in the world trying to free him for a multimillion dollar reward. Multi-rewrites later, Hugo Slater bailed on *S.W.A.T.* and the studio declared they would make the picture on the cheap as an ensemble with young stars. Frank Darabont's rewrite of *Collateral* could have had Hugo Slater playing the contract killer opposite the cab driver but the best Hugo Slater script I ever recommended didn't happen for the big guy and probably wouldn't have worked.

Dollars: Which script was that?

Mersault: *Three Kings* by David O. Russell. When I finished that script, the moment felt holy. I barged into his agent's office to tell him it was the best script I'd ever read for Hugo Slater and he warned me George Clooney was campaigning for the part. At the next Hugo Slater team meeting, I pitched my heart out for *Three Kings* and got shot down by an agent who said he couldn't get past Hugo's thick Latvian accent as a US soldier in Kuwait. I suggested tweaking the script to accommodate Hugo Slater by making his character part of a UN peacekeeping force but that suggestion went nowhere. Hugo Slater became unavailable after his porcine heart valve replacement surgery and it was time for me to do something else at the agency, like putting A-list packages together with my favorite scripts.

Dollars: I've never been packaged by an agency so I can't speak with authority on the subject as perhaps you can.

Mersault: When it happens, it's a miracle. Omniscience puts together a client script with a first-dollar gross producer, the lit department attaches a meaningful director who, by virtue of his track record and relationships, attracts A-list stars from the talent department, creating a package irresistible for a studio to finance and distribute the picture on a worldwide basis. Omniscience is incentivized to do this not just for the multiple commissions from first-dollar gross clients across departments but also to collect a hefty packaging fee from the buyer. Inevitably, I would be requested to write the coverage on a client script brought up in a staff meeting and my opinion was neither needed nor required by the packaging agent.

Dollars: In other words, the agents asked you to sell it, not smell it.

Mersault: Some agents couldn't handle the truth and sent me scripts attached with kneepads. I called those coverages "glow jobs." I had no problem servicing those scripts when I was younger, which may have had something to do with my popularity among the agents.

Dollars: Not to mention your promotion.

SO, YOU ARE A WHORE...NOW WE'RE JUST HAGGLING OVER THE PRICE

Mersault: Look who's back.

Dollars: And quoting Winston Churchill.

NO TELL MOTEL

Screenplay by Aldo Garibaldi

COMMENTS: This is an electrifying sexual thriller that grabs you from the opening image to the last fade out. Reminiscent of BLOOD SIMPLE, the story revolves around a run-down motel, five sketchy characters, and a million dollars in stolen drug money. Double-crossings and double-dealings is all you find at the No Tell Motel. The characters have subtle nuances that only hint of their pasts of pain. The script moves fast and furious, with the two cousins, sex and murder, asserting control over the players. The dialogue drips with the sweaty banter of hardened criminals and abused lovers. The plot twists and turns with surprising revelations and betrayals. No one can be trusted in this tale. In short, this is a hot script about money and murder that deserves our attention.

Dollars: What happens to people who become readers? Thousands of scripts later, are they like my coffee: cold and bitter?

Mersault: The story department was the real mailroom at Omniscience. A few readers became clients. My assistant sold her script *Suffragette City* to Castle Rock and later created the TV show *Doctor Addict*. Another assistant of mine became the show runner of *Modern Nurses*. One of the readers I hired won an Emmy for *Ugly Velma*. Another reader sold his biblical action script *Lazarus* to MGM. Danny Dortmund, who was so tough that if he liked a script it had to be an Oscar winner, sold his screenplay for *My Slut Grandma* to Tri-Star, which I only learned about because *Variety* announced the "ex-Omniscience script reader" Danny Dortmund had sold *My Slut Grandma* for high six-figures in a bidding war with several studios. When Danny Dortmund came into work that day to quit, he went to his reader bin and found twenty scripts, all of them overnights. He went into my office and asked me to reassign those screenplays because he had a meeting with Tri-Star in the morning and he couldn't work for Omniscience anymore. I told Danny Dortmund to go back to his bin for a surprise. Behind the stack of scripts was a bottle of champagne and on the label I'd written: "You're fired."

Dollars: When Paramount submitted *Warlords of Arkadia* to Omniscience for directors, I got my hands on the coverage.

Mersault: Was it Danny Dortmund?

Dollars: It was you. I kept the coverage.

Mersault: You kept the coverage? That's creepy.

WARLORDS OF ARKADIA
Screenplay by Dollars Muttlan

COMMENTS: Problematic and uneven, and yet WARLORDS OF ARKADIA has a fascinating core idea that could be developed into something memorable. Subtitles and pointless narration overwhelm the tale, which is basically the French Revolution reimagined in a future where Earth (renamed Arkadia) is occupied by monster oppressors similar to Marie Antoinette and Louis XVI. During the first sixty pages our hero CLEM is heard only through voice-over, revealing plot details and thoughts about his fellow human rebels. This is a disastrous way to tell a story and script finally drops the narration when Clem is captured by the monstrous warlords. The dialogue has too much stilted, bizarre futuristic lingo when English would have sufficed. Disappointing material, but cool seed of a movie might attract a visually inventive director, a world-creator who could further develop its message about human rights and be skilled enough at action and effects to realize the commercial potential buried inside this hot mess of a script.

Mersault: Well, the movie didn't work but you saved those kids at the *Warlords* premiere.

Dollars: Saving the kids happened at the Chinese Theatre on opening weekend. The premiere at the ArcLight was scarier. My date for the evening was this pretty bank teller from Wells Fargo I'd had a crush on forever. With her, I remembered the ABCs of dating in Los Angeles: Always Bring Cocaine. Paramount sent a limo, not a stretch, but Wells Fargo was impressed. On the red carpet, nobody said a word to me, no executive from the studio hugged me, and there wasn't a soul inside the Cinerama Dome when we took our seats. I hadn't seen the movie. I wasn't invited to the set during filming. All I knew was they cast the movie with some big star from Germany and surrounded him with a bunch of weird names that if you added up all their star power combined, it wouldn't make any goddamn sense. As soon as the movie began, I started to sink in my seat. It was so awful I was on the floor hiding from Wells Fargo, who was wiping her nose and shoveling popcorn in her mouth like she was watching *Empire Strikes Back* or something. Usually people stay in their seats at premieres out of respect, not this crowd. The spaceships looked like toys. The audience was howling at the dialogue. At one point, after a particularly embarrassing scene of the lead actress delivering an excruciating amount of exposition, an audience member shouted out: "Show us your tits!" Wells Fargo started bleeding all over her popcorn after snorting at something on screen she found hilarious. Last line of the movie, which I did not write, had the hero announcing to his half-naked mutant girlfriend, "I'm off to my next adventure." As my sole writing credit flashed on the screen, Wells Fargo was hemorrhaging in the ladies room and the six people left in the Dome bolted for the exits.

Mersault: I've been to some crazy themed premieres where people skip the movie and show up for the open bar or the In-N-Out Burger truck serving double-doubles.

Dollars: I'm not sure what the theme was that night. We had go-go dancers with neon pasties and *Warlords* ice sculptures. A lit manager came up to me, squeezed my shoulder, and said, "Good luck!" I never saw Wells Fargo again.

Mersault: She pulled a French exit?

Dollars: I changed banks. Opening weekend I went to The Grove, bought a ticket to the matinee, and decided I didn't want to be the only one in the theatre so I got my money back and bought a ticket to the next showtime. I walked around the Farmer's Market, bought a bottle of hot sauce, ate something at the food court, and found my theatre at The Grove was empty again. I walked out and drove to the Chinese. I sat down and saw about two rows filled with people: an elderly couple, Korean teenagers wearing suits and ties, a black couple taking their two very young kids, and some Mexican gangbangers who started cheering when the lights went down. Minutes into the movie, the elderly couple got up to leave, angrily shaking their heads, bothered by the alien beheadings in the opening. The grandfather shouted at everybody, "You people are sick!" as if those folks in the theatre were responsible for green-lighting the picture. One of the Korean gangsters shouted, "Shut the fuck up, Grampa!" The old man paused at the exit doors and yelled back: "Come down and make me, you little bastard!" The Korean kid jumped out of his seat and ran toward Grampa. The black guy tackled the Korean reservoir dog, saving the old man, but infuriating his crew.

The Mexicans threw their drink cups and tubs of popcorn at the Koreans. The black guy's wife went over to a Cholo, waved her fat finger in his face and a gunshot exploded, her blasted hand resembled a molten candle, and her kids screamed like they were next to die. The Koreans fired their semiautos at the Cholos, who whipped out their pistoleros. I crawled on the sticky floor toward the emergency exit when I found the black kids crying for their mommy and daddy. I picked them up into my armpits like footballs, threw myself against the exit door, and got those munchkins out.

Mersault: I saw you interviewed on *Good Day LA* with Jillian and Dorothy Lucey after the Mayor declared Dollars Muttlan Day in your honor.

Dollars: I helped those kids, but I couldn't save the box office. On two thousand screens, *Warlords of Arkadia* grossed three hundred and ninety-eight thousand for the lowest per-screen average of all time. Overseas, ticket sales were just as terrible. In South Korea, the movie was perceived as having anti-Christian messages. No one went to see it in Europe, Japan, Brazil, or Russia. I had a bunch of meetings lined up to hear my *Moose on the Loose* pitch but as soon as *Warlords* shit the bed they all got canceled. My agent stopped returning my phone calls. It was as if I had been cremated. When people did call me back, it was their assistants saying they had to reschedule drinks or lunch and they never called me again. At one point I took too many Ambien, shaved off my eyebrows, and stood outside Omniscience holding a cardboard sign: "Will screenwrite for food."

AFTER I RAPED CYBELLE, I CUT OFF HER FEET

Dollars: Now there's a detail only her murderer would know.

SHE WASN'T THE ONLY ONE

Mersault: Serial killers think they're so smart, don't they?

THEY NEVER CAUGHT ME...DOES THAT MAKE ME A GENIUS

Dollars: No, just a lucky son of a bitch.

WHO WAS YOUR WORST READER?

Mersault: I had a reader once who I thought would be so terrible I took bets around the office he wouldn't last a week. That guy, a former client, a rock star who happened to be homeless, became my ace reader for any overnight request, averaged fifteen scripts a week...and was never late on a coverage...all while raising a teenage son by himself.

Dollars: Knock it off. Your best reader was a homeless guy?

Mersault: I got this phone call from the head of the music department at Omniscience who used to represent this band from the eighties. The agent asked if I would take a few minutes to meet this singer-songwriter who went to Bennington College, a favorite of *LA Times* music critic Robert Hilburn, a brilliant lead vocalist who had fallen on hard times, struggling to raise a young boy by himself, living out of his car and crashing on people's couches. A meeting was set and Steven Tyler's ancestor waltzed into my office, craggy face, longish hair in a bandanna, Concrete Blonde concert T-shirt, unlit cigarette behind his ear, and immediately started telling me about his misfortune. I cut him off to say he had the job as a reader. The rock star said he'd never done script coverage before, and I said something like, "You have a degree from Bennington, it's not brain surgery." The rock star laughed and called me a cool dude and started talking about the time he was on tour with Jetboy and Thelonius Monster and again I cut him off to explain how to write a logline, a one-page summary, an evaluation, and a character breakdown. I gave the rock star *Snakes on a Plane* to cover along with some samples and told him to steal any phrases to make his evaluation seem credible. After two months of living out of his car and getting the hang of writing coverage, the rock star and his son were able to move into a new apartment in the Valley. The best moment was when an agent wanted him to be his exclusive reader. I told the rock star about this request and he couldn't believe an agent at Omniscience trusted his judgment that much. I reminded him he went to Bennington. The worst moment was when another agent called me about his negative review of a client script and ordered the coverage destroyed and the reader fired immediately. I told the agent both directives would be obeyed, not to worry.

Dollars: That's outrageous. The agent made you fire the rock star because he couldn't handle the truth?

Mersault: Who said I fired the rock star? I called him up, explained what happened, and told him to keep doing what he was doing. I explained that since our readers used their initials on coverage and not their names he should just change his reader initials and no one would ever know.

Dollars: Now that's genius. Did he ever write a song about reading scripts?

Mersault: He wrote and recorded this amazing album while he read for Omniscience. My favorite song was about trying to date when you're homeless called "Back Seat Driver."

MAYBE I SHOULD WRITE SCRIPTS

Mersault: I would love to read one of your scripts.

Dollars: Mighty generous of you.

Mersault: See, now he's quiet.

BOMB ON BOARD
Screenplay by Hans Grohl

COMMENTS: Exhilarating thriller that never lets up and delivers on its enticing premise set on a city bus that's timed to explode if the speedometer drops below fifty-five miles an hour. LAPD bomb squad member HANK REVIS boards the doomed bus, works with the frightened passengers, and tries to figure a way out while his aging partner, MEEKS, discovers the mastermind is a disgruntled ex-bomb squad cop named WINSTON WHITE. Meeks gets killed, but Hank saves the passengers after a wild, incredible ride on a hurtling booby-trapped bus from hell that ends on a satisfying note. Piled on with external obstacles, Hank isn't given much of a character (it would have been nice if he fought some inner demons...), but the script simply moves too fast to attempt development. Mad bomber White is a solid, stereotypical villain who's lost his mind (along with his left thumb). There's a fun love interest for Hank in the attractive twenty-something JANIE, who is forced to take the wheel when the bus driver is wounded. Fast and frisky cop thriller demands our attention.

Dollars: As a reader you were more like Caesar than a Christian: thumbs up, you got packaged, thumbs down, death.

Mersault: I never saw what I did for a living as judge, jury, and executioner. Sometimes agents requested me to write the coverage for their client's script because they wanted the franchise. Sometimes I was asked to help clients tweak their scripts before they turned in their assignments to the studios. Sometimes a TV writer client had a pitch for a movie idea and the agent would set me up in the Alvarez conference room like a studio executive and the client would come in at the appointed hour and pitch me cold. One time I ordered lobster rolls from the Beverly Wilshire Hotel for a working lunch with Patrick Swayze and we developed a treatment for his dream project about Arabian horses. The story department at Omniscience was not where scripts went to die, it was where movies began.

Dollars: I had no idea this happened inside an agency. When I was with Insanely Creative, my agents would point out a typo or advise me to change the title of my werewolf comedy to *Tastes Like Chicken.*

Mersault: Word got around the motion picture department that I gave great memo, so I started developing client scripts instead of writing coverage. An agent called and asked if I'd heard of a novel called *Leaving Laughlin,* and I said, "Of course," thinking of driving Miss Daisy, and the agent said the author wanted a few tips about writing a screenplay and would I meet with him?

Dollars: Did you get lobster rolls from the Beverly Wilshire?

Mersault: John O'Brien wasn't looking for a free meal. He wanted serious advice how to write screenplays so he could maybe make a living at it since he was always broke. Hollywood had optioned his book and he said he was worried they were going to "*Pretty Woman*-ize" his tragic ending. John O'Brien showed me his unpublished novel, *Zipper Lessons,* and then we set out to work on this idea he had for a movie called *Neon Money*, this really ambitious, vaguely sci-fi story about a future where fascist corporations run America and a giant food company like Beatrice has taken over the government and they carry out political assassinations via drive-by shootings. I thought the tale was wild and encouraged him to write the fuck out of it and come back to me with a finished script. A month or two later, John O'Brien greeted me in the lobby of Omniscience all excited with this two-hundred page tome called *Neon Money*. I read it a couple times, wrote the coverage, and called him up to say: "Okay, John. Now the real work begins. You ready to rewrite your script?" And John O'Brien was like, "They can pay me to fix it." I couldn't convince him to change a word. He thought what he had done was just brilliant. I promoted the script to a shameless literary agent who would throw anything at the studios only to be told there was "no money" in *Neon Money*. I lost touch with John O'Brien until I caught his obituary in the *LA Times*. I went to a reading of his posthumous novel at Book Soup and met someone who said she used to be John O'Brien's attorney and she promised to send me a PDF of *Neon Money* but she never did.

WHAT WILL BE WRITTEN ON YOUR TOMBSTONE?

Mersault: He passed.

NEON MONEY
Screenplay by John O'Brien

COMMENTS: Paranoid, ambitious, uneven conspiracy thriller that needs to build on its driving storyline and create a more satisfying climax. Five years after the mysterious death of his girlfriend, DENNIS VAIL discovers a sinister conglomerate named ROSCO has taken over the country's public works in a capitalistic plot to overthrow the Constitution. Script starts out strongly, establishing Dennis, Rosco, and the other players who will later contribute to the story. Vaguely futuristic, the ambitious setting is one of script's strongest suits, grounded in economic reality without fancy special effects like BLADE RUNNER. Dialogue and characters are a notch above the usual list of suspects. There's nervy tension when people around Dennis start to die (it's a stroke to have them perish by drive-by shootings). The resolution suggests Rosco has become so big it has started to devour itself and will ultimately be destroyed. But there's no sense that big, bad Rosco is on the course to self-immolation. Dennis must strike the blow that, even if it's just a chink in Rosco's armor, will start a chain reaction of destruction (in other words, he must cut off the head of the Hydra). As written, it's not enough when MUNSON declares the inevitable end of his company and then gives Dennis a golden parachute to walk away. The fight against Rosco needs to be bloodier, stronger, more exciting (the best the anti-Rosco forces can do is shut down the power of the headquarters tower—it's a metaphorical victory, not visceral enough). Without being hokey or using familiar, tired action smoke and mirrors, there should be another way to pull off script's frightening premise with an exciting, satisfying climax worthy of its ambitious concept. In short, this is special material that requires deeper thought.

YOU WROTE HIS OBITUARY WITH
THAT COVERAGE

Dollars: What do you remember most about the Harry Hunt regime when he took over the agency in nineteen ninety-nine?

Mersault: The Harry Hunt decade was a blur, but if I could single out one memory it would have to be after surviving Y2K, enjoying a threesome in a limo with those waitresses from House of Chan Dara, most of our clothes still on, drunk out of our minds, taking Sunset Boulevard all the way to the Pacific Coast Highway and then discovering the next day in the very first Harry Hunt Wednesday morning motion picture staff meeting a long incriminating stain on my suit pants that would have made Monica Lewinsky's blue dress proud.

Dollars: An auspicious beginning to the decade.

Mersault: It was all downhill after that, as Soderbergh famously said when he won the Palme d'Or for *sex, lies, and videotape*. There was a brief purge, all my mentors left the company, and I got more involved with the agent training program, sharing my knowledge about the business and material with trainees desperate to get out of the mailroom during their time in the story department rotation. Sometimes I took them to staff meetings so they could get a glimpse of their future.

Dollars: Why was it downhill after the limo ride?

Mersault: It wasn't downhill exactly, but internally the regime change was a momentum-killer for me. Management tasked me with the challenging assignment of supervising the creation of an integrated database that linked the coverage library with our internal studio/independent projects panels and a new template that identified branded entertainment opportunities for Omniscience corporate clients.

Dollars: Sorry, I was texting. What do you mean, supervising an integrated database to identify branded entertainment?

Mersault: No longer was I a packaging gladiator in the deathsport known as the movie business. The Harry Hunt regime made me a weapons designer in the IT Department overseeing the construction of the Purina Pet Chow Death Star. I needed to vent, so I wrote a novel about a script reader at a talent agency who gets radicalized and turns into a suicide bomber.

Dollars: I self-published a sex manual called *Make Him Marry You.* What did your colleagues say about representing your Hollywood novel?

Mersault: Omniscience passed. The feedback from the New York office was that no publisher would want it because they said every character in my novel was reprehensible and only women bought fiction.

Dollars: Did you tell the New York office to sell it and not smell it?

Mersault: I did, actually. The agent said she wasn't a cocktail waitress and hung up on me. I decided to e-mail query letters directly to publishers. My query letters got rejection letters. The novel remained unread and unpublished until I got one request for the manuscript from this tiny mystery press in Portland, Maine. I sent off the book and went to a staff meeting where agents in the motion picture department reported on what the studios were doing and which projects were heating up when a senior agent complained about their lack of a point of view about material. "The only person in this room," declared this well-respected literary agent, "who knows how to read a script is Larry

Mersault." The room got real quiet. On the set of *The Grey Area*, Franklin Brauner told me a story about the time he passed on this hostage negotiator script that described a pause on the page as a defecating silence. Franklin said when he suggested to the writer's manager that maybe the defecating silence be changed to something less bizarre, the lit manager became indignant and said, "I stand by my client. He's not changing a word." Franklin leaned back in his director's chair and wondered out loud, "A defecating silence. How would I shoot that?"

Dollars: So when the agent made that comment about you in that staff meeting it was met with a defecating silence?

Mersault: Exactly. I left that staff meeting with the eyes of more than a few agents on my back. I got an e-mail from an agent who represented a financier in Amsterdam and a Dutch director whose last film was nominated for a Best Foreign Film Oscar and they wanted to make a spaghetti western in Spain where Sergio Leone shot *The Good, The Bad and The Ugly* with Clint Eastwood and they were looking for a script to finance as a six-million-dollar European coproduction. I sent over my favorite unproduced Western called *Lucky Trails* and then another agent asked me for an available martial arts family comedy with kids. He had a client who would bring the action, the material had to bring the comedy, what did I have sitting on the shelf? I recommended an old favorite that fit the bill called *My Neighbor the Weirdo* by our clients who wrote the Amanda Bynes reincarnation comedy *You Again?* Then one of our freelance script readers walked into my office with her hair on fire and said, "I just read a great script with a terrible title about a White House chef who leads a double life as an assassin." I closed my door and hit the couch and an hour later I was calling the unrepped writer of *Abbatoir Parsley* to set a meeting-slash-coffee. My reader was absolutely correct in her assessment, and when I told her I met the screenwriter and landed him an agent she insisted they change the title to *Executive Orders*. We did, and that script she flagged sold to Universal for three million dollars and topped The Black List.

Dollars: So, wait. If you didn't have an agent, how did your novel get published?

Mersault: I went to work one morning and opened an e-mail from Sally, the acquisitions editor of a publishing house called Peach Point Press in Atlanta. According to Sally, I would never get published, no publisher cared about the sausage factory called Hollywood, and I shouldn't be wasting people's time with silly query letters that fill up their inboxes. I deleted the e-mail and went about my day resisting the urge to send her a polite "thank you for considering me" response. I came back from lunch and clicked open an e-mail from Scooby Press in Portland, Maine, the only publisher that ever asked to read the manuscript: "Dear Larry, I have read your novel and I would like to publish it. Please contact me so I can send you a contract. Sincerely, Tom Everett, publisher, Scooby Press." Thinking he was working some scam where I would have to pay him for the privilege of publishing my novel, I called the number and when he answered, I said, "Mr. Everett, you're real." I asked him about Scooby's editing process, and he said, "No notes." I undeleted the message from Peach Point Press, forwarded the Scooby Press e-mail and wrote, "Dear Sally, Life works in mysterious ways. See below." I never got a response.

Dollars: What did your parents say about the novel?

Mersault: They read the four-hundred-and-eighty-nine-page rough draft. Mom was about fifty pages ahead of Dad when she put the book down and said, "Where did we go wrong?"

WAS THERE EVER A MOMENT WHERE YOU THOUGHT YOU WOULD GET FIRED?

Mersault: I got rid of an intern not knowing his father was best friends with the Chairman Emeritus of Omniscience. I received a phone call from the Chairman Emeritus himself, not an uncommon event since he had requested my reader reports for years, and the Chairman Emeritus went bananas: "How dare you besmirch me? I heard you fired so-and-so and now you go around besmirching my reputation?" I stood up at my desk and lost control of my bladder. I denied that I had ever besmirched his reputation, that obviously he had gotten an earful from a disgruntled employee I had just terminated. Urine was running down my leg when the Chairman Emeritus lowered his voice and said he knew I had a tough job, how termination was always difficult, General Motors had just fired three hundred thousand workers at their factories, keep up the great work running the story department, and by the way he needed me to review a musical about bag ladies due first thing in the morning. I hung up the phone, went home to change, and dropped off my pants on the way back to Beverly Hills. I had lived to fight another day.

Dollars: Sounds like you kept your dry cleaner busy.

WHAT WAS THE OMNISCIENCE/ RAGNARÖK MERGER LIKE?

Mersault: When the Rodney King riots broke out, the air was on fire, palm trees were burning, and I remember driving from Hollywood to Beverly Hills in my convertible with a baseball bat between the seats in case somebody tried to jack me. That's what the merger felt like: all of the above. The rumors were flying every day. We represented the youngest director in the world who had just been slimed at the Nickelodeon Kids' Choice Awards when his agent announced in a staff meeting that the kid auteur was looking for a family comedy. I sent over *My Neighbor the*

Weirdo and a week later the youngest director in the world declared he wanted to make it his next picture. Then I heard the martial artist Hop Woo wanted to play the Weirdo. Omniscience attached a first-dollar gross producer client who wanted to make a movie his kids could see and the package sold to Summit as a green-lit thirty-million-dollar movie. At the height of Nikki Finke hourly updating lists of agents who were toast, pending Federal approval of the union, inside a staff meeting of motion picture agents it was business as usual, projects being promoted or dissed, clients needing to go to work, no discussion whatsoever about the agency down the street when the lights dimmed and a fake poster appeared on the screen for an upcoming Hop Woo movie called *My Neighbor the Weirdo*. Applause. Directed by the youngest auteur in the world. More cheers. Total writer, producer, director, Hop Woo commissions plus packaging fee: a million dollars. Then the last shout-out appeared on screen: A Larry Mersault Special. Standing ovation. The merger with Ragnarök was approved by the Obama Administration and it was time to purge.

Dollars: When did you find out you made the cut?

Mersault: The day of the axe was like, if you got a phone call from someone in management or human resources, the jig was up. If you didn't get a call by six o'clock that day, you were safe. My assistant brought me the trades that morning and I noticed an article in *The Hollywood Reporter* announcing a spaghetti western called *Lucky Trails* with a Dutch director would be shooting in Almeria, Spain where Sergio Leone made his films and I thought, *That's my favorite Western script, how come nobody bothered to tell me?* At the end of the article it said the project had been packaged by Omniscience/Ragnarök's Larry Mersault. I showed my assistant the article and she still didn't believe we were safe until it was five fifty-nine and we left the office for the day.

WHAT'S THE WORST DATE YOU'VE EVER HAD?

Mersault: You first. My lips are tired.

Dollars: I went on a couple dates with a news reporter from KCAL-9 pretending to be "Nigel from Liverpool" with this bullshit cockney accent. We were fooling around at her place when I heard someone making noises upstairs. KCAL-9 said I could sleep with her roommate later but not at the same time, and I said, "Can't we all just get along?" And she said, "I live with my mom." And I said, in my real voice, "Oh, hell no," and walked out.

Mersault: I once got set up by my assistant with her friend Nancy who worked in the music department. Our date was a disaster from the moment we were driving around Thai Town looking for a parking space. All Nancy talked about was how much she hated Hollywood and compared herself to Dorothy in *The Wizard of Oz* having to deal with cowardly lions and men with no brains. Everybody, including me, she said, was a streetwalker trolling the yellow brick road. I was holding open the door when Nancy freaked out about the B health code rating in the window and refused to enter the Thai restaurant: "I don't eat at B's." So we drove around looking for a place to eat, despising each other, but hungry enough to pretend we were still on a date so we could eat something. She was texting her friends the whole time I was driving until I found a parking spot right in front of this place called Toi on Sunset. She ignored the A rating and entered the restaurant with a bad attitude. I ordered two bottles of hot sake and asked Nancy what she was having. We got some naked shrimp, an order of Tod Mun Pla, pineapple fried rice, and Singha beer. I asked her about working in the music department. Nancy said she liked going to clubs to check out the new bands but the best part of her job was hanging out with clients. When Nancy said she seduced an infamous guitarist in an elevator, I told her, "That guy is a heroin addict." Nancy asked me if I was religious. I said I believed in a radio god and parking angels. Nancy, a nonbelieving Jew, said she didn't understand. I explained that whenever I needed a parking space like the one we had miraculously found tonight, I made a point of thanking my parking angels. Whenever a song came on the car radio that I loved, I always looked out the windshield and thanked the radio god for playing my favorite tune. "Let me get this straight," she said, "you have a radio god who plays the songs you want and angels who give you parking spaces. Why don't you pray to a money god or happiness angels?" She called me a fish-eyed fool and ended our date to meet her friends at The Viper Room. "Let me get this straight," I said, "you sleep with junkies but you don't eat at restaurants that get a B from the health department. Why don't you go fuck yourself?"

WHAT'S THE WORST THING YOU'VE EVER DONE?

Mersault: I haven't killed anyone. A few projects, maybe.

Dollars: Have you done anything in your career that no one knows about, that made a difference in someone's life?

Mersault: I once got a phone call from my best friend from childhood, an LAPD detective, asking me if I knew anybody on the TV show *Extreme Makeover: Home Edition.* A patrol officer from the seventy-seventh precinct, Ange

Colletti, was shot on duty and paralyzed from the waist down. Her house wasn't equipped for her disability and the family was trying to raise money through bake sales and donations but it would never be enough for Officer Colletti. My friend asked me if I had any contacts in reality TV who could give him the number to the front desk of *Extreme Makeover: Home Edition* so he could nominate Officer Colletti for the show. I told my friend that wasn't the best way to make it happen. So I called the reality TV agent at Omniscience who packaged the show, who put me in touch with the creator of *Extreme Makeover*. Months later, my friend from the LAPD called and said he had somebody next to him who wanted to tell me something. It was Officer Colletti saying, "Thank you, thank you, thank you." When I watched the episode of *Extreme Makeover: Home Edition*, Officer Colletti and her family waved at the camera from inside their renovated wheelchair-accessible house, surrounded by smiling neighbors and applauding officers in blue. I waved back.

SATANIC
Screenplay by David Kahane

COMMENTS: Intriguing serial killer tale unfolds with the same brushstrokes as MONSTER and ZODIAC. Same room tone of PRISONERS. While there have been several films about RICHARD RAMIREZ, this feels definitive. We never see the murders. We see Ramirez growing up in a horrible, tortured environment of abuse and drugs and murders committed against his own family members. Throughout the whole story, his longtime girlfriend, ALICE, thinks Ramirez is going to propose to her, unaware that her BF is the "Night Stalker." Sometimes, script plays like it's her movie, only instead of a clichéd detective pursuing the serial killer, playing cat and mouse, here it's Alice who orbits Ramirez's world, afraid/ashamed of him, fearful of her lonely future without him, suspecting the worst, then discovering the awful truth. Material is not a suspenseful thriller like SILENCE OF THE LAMBS nor is it about the catharsis of catching a killer and the relief of ending his reign; it's all about the damaged people associated with the Night Stalker while he was terrorizing a city.

PAINT A PICTURE OF A WRITER'S LONGEVITY FROM WRITING SAMPLE TO DEATH

Mersault: From writing sample to death? Okay, you're a senior at the most expensive private school in Santa Monica. You're best friends with the children of studio heads and agents and showrunners. You write a screenplay about these seventeen-year-old mean girls who join a Latino street gang in East LA that gets into the hands of an executive at New Line Cinema through an acquaintance who's an intern there and the script sells for a hundred grand. You get an agent because everyone in the business heard about your script sale and wants to meet you but you have to graduate high school first and forget about going to college when your first meeting at New Line is the day after graduation with an Oscar-winning documentary director and eight executives in the room. Another writer, more seasoned than you, is assigned to do a page-one rewrite and you never work on it again. When your movie comes out years later under a different title, it barely resembles your original premise. Your afternoons are spent taking meetings with creative executives who want you to fix their projects in development but never actually hire you. After a year or two of trying to get paid to rewrite a script your agent sets you up in television with a blind pilot deal where you pitch a show about ballerina mean girls that gets shot and lands on the NBC fall schedule only to be canceled after two low-rated episodes. Fingers are pointed, but you're only nineteen, and every nitwit at every network wants your next show. Then you are approached by a French producer-director-mogul to adapt a novel about a mute stripper because he's a huge fan of your work. That script gets made before the New Line thing but it's a Canal Plus TV movie and never plays in the States so it's like the movie doesn't exist. Back in LA your agent sets up a round of meetings with executives who want to meet the writer who sold that script to New Line when she was twelve and you don't correct them in the room. You write a script for yourself to direct about a homeless girl who falls for a law student and the film gets into Sundance and after you win the Grand Jury Prize everyone at the studios wants to meet you because now they want you to fix their projects by rewriting their screenplays to direct. Then you're in a light plane flown by your uncle and you die in a fiery crash when it inexplicably plunges into an apartment building in the Fairfax district. Dollars, stop texting on your phone!

WHERE'S THE SEQUEL TO THE LAST WEDDING?

Dollars: You mean my movie that won a couple of Silver Unicorns at the Estepona Film Festival?

Mersault: Did you like directing?

Dollars: It damn near killed me. I wrote the script in a month during the time I was separated from my first wife and I was sleeping on an air mattress at the house of my best friend who officiated the wedding. I imagined what would have happened if my ex-wife had killed herself rather than filed for divorce. What if I got engaged and my new fiancée was possessed by the vengeful spirit of my dead ex-wife? I wrote the first scene in the script where the crazy wife is in the kitchen and says she's gone off her meds and wants to have children and when my character tells her he wants a divorce, she grabs a butcher's knife and slits her throat in front of him.

Mersault: That script must have been difficult to write.

Dollars: Are you kidding? This thing wrote itself after that opening scene. I had a scene at the altar where the possessed bride gives the scariest wedding vow in the history of wedding movies. I designed it as a found footage movie where everything unfolds through the camera of the wedding videographer, the hotel security cameras, or someone's iPhone. A line producer I knew broke it down and said he could see the picture being made for three hundred and sixty thousand dollars. No stars, just talent. I sold six units at sixty thousand dollars each to a lawyer, his sister, a rabbi, a professional golfer, and the wealthy parents of my new girlfriend, who wanted to play the small but pivotal role of the demon ex-wife. I needed them to buy two units so I gave her the part. In preproduction, my lead actor dropped out to shoot a Joel Silver TV pilot in Australia so I cast myself as the groom opposite my girlfriend, who told her parents she should star as the possessed bride if they were going to invest that much money in the movie. Over everyone's objection, I agreed to the change of casting. I slept maybe two hours a night for eighteen days. We stopped having sex when we started shooting and I don't think we ever did again. I wanted to quit by the end of my first day. My girlfriend was such a diva on set she drove away our DP at the end of the first week. I promoted the gaffer to finish the film after he said he could handle it. Horrendous decision on my part. It gave me an appreciation for how hard it is to make a terrible movie. We did not get into Sundance. We did not get accepted to South by Southwest. I invited the investors to join me for the premiere in Estepona but no one was talking to anyone at that point so I went to Spain by myself. *The Last Wedding* ended up winning a Silver Unicorn for best screenplay and the Manuel Orantes best B-movie award.

Mersault: What did your investors think about that?

Dollars: The investors took the picture away from me and signed over *The Last Wedding* to a distributor called Cinema Shares, which was funny because they didn't share a dime and they don't put movies in cinemas.

Mersault: Would you direct again if you had the chance?

Dollars: In a New York second.

Mersault: Are you working on a new script?

Dollars: This lit manager I know sent my script over to Omniscience and the reader killed it.

Mersault: I hope you were getting a blowjob while you were reading the coverage.

Dollars: You called my script an abortion in the opening kicker sentence–

LIFT OFF

Screenplay by Dix Steele

COMMENTS: Highly derivative of APOLLO 13 and THE ROCK, this abortion of a script aspires to be an event action flick and fails so utterly in every aspect of screenwriting, calling this a DIE HARD knock-off is an insult to John McClane. For DQ, there is nothing about LIFT OFF or astronaut HARRISON that merits his consideration or, for that matter, any of our top clients. Offering the barest of character depth, script has no shame claiming the Challenger disaster was engineered by the US gov't, which drives the villain astronaut DASH to hijack a black ops military space shuttle and hold the world hostage with its nuclear cargo. Superficial script boasts stick figures for characters and banal action-movie banter between Dash and Harrison as they go mano a mano in outer space. Stale popcorn script doesn't deserve our attention and should be declared highly toxic for our clients.

Mersault: Dollars, you did not invite me to your class so you could lay the blame of your failure at my feet.

Dollars: What if there never was a class?

Mersault: I don't get it.

THE COLLEGE FIRED ME LAST MONTH

Mersault: Did you text that? Let me see–

Dollars: Hey! Give me back my iPhone!

I KNOW WHO KILLED CYBELLE

Mersault: It was you, texting the whole time.

WHAT WILL BE WRITTEN ON YOUR TOMBSTONE?

Mersault: Dollars! Put away that fucking hammer!

Dollars: Murder is easy–

Mersault: Unlock this door!

Dollars: The movie business? Tough racket.

[recording ends]

CALL SHEET

Bruce Wagner
Miley Cyrus
Michael Tolkin
Tyson Cornell
Jerry Stahl
The Human Centipede
Lauren
Josh Gilbert
JD and Elisabeth
Reinhard and Marilee
Sara and Adam
Dennis and Molly
Greathouse
Christopher
Galloway
Michael Rose
André Øvredal
James Cox
Gasmer
Ptak
Simpson
Burnham
Rifkin
Nicole
Morley
King
Mom and Dad
Barbara and Brian
Jonathan and Prescott
Spencer and Logan and Grayson
Jessie and Brian and Alex
Samantha

CALL SHEET

Bruce Wagner
Miley Cyrus
Michael Tolkin
Tyson Cornell
Jerry Stahl
The Human Centipede
Lauren
Josh Gilbert
JD and Elisabeth
Reinhard and Marilee
Sara and Adam
Dennis and Molly
Greathouse
Christopher
Galloway
Michael Rose
André Øvredal
James Cox
Gasmer
Ptak
Simpson
Burnham
Rifkin
Nicole
Morley
King
Mom and Dad
Barbara and Brian
Jonathan and Prescott
Spencer and Logan and Grayson
Jessie and Brian and Alex
Samantha